# LIGHTNING
## Fighting the Living Dead

SHAUN HARBINGER

**Lightning: Fighting the Living Dead**
Copyright © 2015 Shaun Harbinger
All rights reserved.

# THE UNDEAD RAIN SERIES

Rain: Rise of the Living Dead
Storm: Survival in the Land of the Dead
Lightning: Fighting the Living Dead
Wildfire: Destruction of the Dead

# CHAPTER 1

BACKED AWAY FROM LUCY, my heart pounding. I couldn't believe what I was seeing. How had she been bitten? How had she gotten a syringe of the vaccine? How as I supposed to help her?

"Leave…me…alone," she murmured.

I couldn't just leave her in the storeroom; it didn't seem right. But if I tried to move her to one of the bedrooms, what would she do? Would she freak out if I tried to get her to her feet?

I wasn't sure it made a difference to her where she was; she was probably unaware of her surroundings. But I didn't want to leave her here curled up on the floor. I approached her. "Lucy." I kept my voice low, almost a whisper, trying to soothe her.

She shrank away from me. "Leave…me…alone." She looked frightened, her eyes wide, darting from me to the

1

room. If my presence was going to make her try to escape, I should just leave her here. I didn't want her running up to the deck in a blind panic and falling overboard.

I turned to leave the room, colliding with a shelf in my haste. A pile of Sail to Your Destiny t-shirts fell to the floor. I got out of there and closed the door. As long as she wasn't disturbed, Lucy should stay where she was, compelled by the virus to stay in a safe place.

The virus. It was running through her blood, changing her. If it remained in her system for four days, Lucy would become a monster, a hybrid. What would I do then? Kill her? No, I couldn't do that. No matter what happened to her, I could never do that.

I went back up the stairs, through the living area, and out onto the aft deck. On *The Lucky Escape*, Sam, Jax, Tanya, and Johnny were waiting for me to reappear. They must have seen something in my face, because Jax looked concerned.

"Alex, what's wrong?" she asked.

"It's Lucy. She's been bitten. She took the vaccine and left me a note saying that she's been bitten today." Saying it out loud made it seem worse somehow. I sat wearily on the bench that ran around the perimeter of the deck and put my head in my hands. There was no way out of this.

A few seconds later, Jax and Sam came onboard *The Big Easy*, stepping over from the *Escape*.

"I'm sorry, man," Sam said. He spread his big hands as if he was unsure what to say after that.

LIGHTNING

Jax sat on the bench next to me and put her arm around my shoulder. "Alex, I'm so sorry. I know how much you were looking forward to seeing Lucy again. It's terrible that it has to end like this."

"It hasn't ended yet," I said. "She was bitten today. That means she has four days before she turns."

She patted my shoulder as if she were consoling an upset child who had just learned that Santa isn't real. "We've all seen the hybrids. We know what happened to those soldiers after they got bitten. There's nothing we can do for Lucy in the next four days that's going to stop the same thing happening to her."

"Jesus," Sam said, "Way to go easy on the poor guy."

Jax sighed. "I'm only being realistic, Sam."

My mind reeled from shock and tried to find a solution at the same time. I couldn't think straight. But I had to, for Lucy's sake. I wasn't going to just float around on the waves while she lay curled up in the storeroom becoming a monster.

I looked at Jax. "You said you were going to try to find Apocalypse Island."

She nodded.

"Maybe they have a cure for this. You said yourself that if anyone had a cure, it was the scientists on that island."

"Yes, I did. But it's a secret government research facility, Alex. They aren't just going to hand you the cure. And that's assuming a cure even exists. Don't you think

3

that if they had developed an antivirus, they would be handing it out by now?"

"But they might have it," I said, desperate to believe that there was something I could do for Lucy. I couldn't accept a situation with no hope.

"Hey, we're going there anyway," Sam said. "There's no harm in letting Alex come too."

Jax nodded. "Just as long as he doesn't expect some sort of miracle. We're not even sure we'll find the island."

"We got a good lead on the coordinates when we were doing the story on the island," Sam said. "We have a chance to find it. That's all Alex is asking for, a chance."

He was right. The slightest glimmer of hope would be enough to motivate me into action. I needed something to hang on to, even if it was just a thin thread.

"We should get moving," he said. "Do you want me to stay on here with you, man?"

I nodded. "Yeah, I'd like that."

Jax climbed back onto the *Escape*. Sam took a seat on the bench where she had been sitting, and I climbed the ladder to the bridge. Lucy had lashed the wheel into a fixed position using cord. I untied it, thankful that she was smart enough to take the necessary actions to get *The Big Easy* here before she succumbed to the virus. If she'd gone off course, I would have wasted precious time searching for her.

I followed *The Lucky Escape* north along the coast. We kept a couple of miles offshore, aware that the army was fortifying positions at marinas and docks. We didn't want to be taking fire from artillery on the cliffs, or tank on the beaches.

Sam remained mostly quiet, apart from an occasional, "Everything's going to be okay, man," or "Don't' worry, dude, we'll find that island." I knew he meant well but my natural pessimism shook off his kind words. I could only think about what would happen if we didn't find Apocalypse Island. And even if we did, what if there was no cure? What if nothing could be done for Lucy?

The thread of hope was already unraveling in my mind.

We sailed north for three hours. The sunny afternoon became a cool evening as we reached the coast of Scotland. I switched on the running lights and asked Sam to get me a sweater. When he came back with it, and one for himself, he handed it to me quietly. I realized he must have fetched them from the storeroom and seen Lucy curled up in the corner. His earlier optimism seemed to have disappeared now that he had seen her with his own eyes.

A northerly wind whispered coldly over the decks, and the chill seemed to reach my bones.

The *Escape* changed course, heading away from the coast into the open sea. I followed, watching the stars appear in the darkening sky. Seeing the changes in the environment reminded me that time was running out with each passing second.

Half an hour later, the *Escape* stopped moving forward and began drifting. I cut the engines to *The Big Easy* and drifted alongside.

Tanya poked her head out from the *Escape*'s bridge. "This should be the place."

I looked over the choppy sea. The sky was a deep, dark blue, and an almost full moon hung over the water, illuminating everything with a spectral silver light. If there was an island around here, it should be visible.

I grabbed a pair of binoculars and climbed down to the aft deck. Sam was leaning over the safety railing, squinting into the distance.

Moving past him, I went to the sun deck and used the binoculars to confirm what I most feared. There was no island here. We were drifting in the middle of nowhere. I lowered the binoculars.

"I see something," Johnny shouted. "Over there." He pointed toward the dark horizon.

Bringing up the binoculars to my eye again, I scanned the area he had pointed at. I couldn't see anything until I adjusted the focus, and then I saw a dark shape. It was a long way from our location and it wasn't necessarily an island. It could be a large ship drifting out there in the night.

"Let's go," Tanya said, disappearing into the bridge again. *The Escape*'s engines roared into life.

As I walked past him on the aft deck, Sam was grinning. "I told you, man. Next stop Apocalypse Island."

LIGHTNING

I smiled thinly at him. Even if it was an island out there and not a ship, there was no guarantee it was the place we were looking for. I wished I had Sam's eternal optimism but I climbed up to the bridge with no expectations. I had learned a long time ago that the only way you couldn't be disappointed was if you expected nothing.

The sky was almost fully dark as we reached the island. Surrounded by steep cliffs and treacherous rocks jutting from the sea like claws, it wasn't a welcoming place. Atop the cliffs, I could see what looked like a pine forest. There was no sign of life apart from those trees and a few gulls riding the chilly breeze.

The radio crackled and Tanya's voice said, "Nothing much over here except rocks. "We should go around and take a look at the seaward side."

I picked up the hand mic and said, "Yeah, okay."

As we sailed around the island, staying clear of the rocks, I watched the cliffs for any sign that there might be people here. The woods up there looked dense. The cliff edges were vertical, sheer rock faces in most parts, impossible to climb up without the proper equipment.

I was beginning to think we had chanced upon a deserted piece of rock and trees when our course took us to the other end of the island. It was a very different story here; it looked like explosives and cutting tools had been used to build a road that led down from the trees to a small pebbly beach. Reaching out into the sea from the beach was a long dock. Formed of huge concrete blocks, it looked like it could withstand the roughest seas.

There were four boats moored at the dock. Two of them were large yachts, forty-two footers if my estimation was correct. Alongside them, two smaller boats with outboard motors rolled on the waves, covered with dark blue tarps.

Tanya's voice came over the radio. "I'd say this is the place, Alex." Her voice was calm.

Although the sight of the boats meant that this probably was Apocalypse Island, it didn't mean we could just go strolling up those cliffs and ask for a cure for Lucy. The security for these types of places was strict even before the zombie apocalypse; now, it probably worked on a shoot first, ask questions later basis.

"Got any ideas?" Tanya asked.

I had to admit that I didn't. I hadn't thought ahead this far. We had no idea what we would be walking into if we went along that road into the woods. "Maybe a couple of us should check it out before we all go blundering in," I said.

"Yeah, sounds good. Why don't you tie up on that dock? You and Sam can take a look around. I'll keep the *Escape* out at sea, just in case."

Her plan was logical. There was no need to risk both boats. Sending *The Big Easy* in to the dock while the *Escape* held back was the safest plan for everyone. Well, it was safest for everyone except Sam and me, the sacrificial lambs.

I relayed the plan to Sam, shouting down to him from the bridge. He gave me a thumbs-up sign, said, "Cool, man," and began to get the ropes ready for docking.

I took the *Easy* in nice and slow, keeping her at the end of the dock, next to one of the forty-two footers, in case we needed to escape here in a hurry. Sam sorted the ropes, and I went down the ladder to the aft deck. "What about weapons?" I asked him.

"Yeah, bring two bats," he said, his eyes on the dark road that led up through the cliffs.

I grabbed two bats, threw him one of them, and stepped off the boat and onto the concrete dock.

He grinned at me. "Let's go find some scientists."

As we walked along the dock, the moon gazed down at us with an unemotional, uncaring face.

# CHAPTER 2

THE ROAD AT THE END of the dock was wide enough for vehicles and had been topped with asphalt. As we walked along it, I expected a Jeep to come barreling toward us, full of armed men shining flashlights in our faces. I had seen too many movies; this wasn't the secret lair of a James Bond villain, it was an island that belonged to the British government. We weren't looking for a man sitting in a chair stroking a white cat, but a team of scientists.

Sam had been quiet since we'd left the *Easy*, which was unlike him, but was probably the best idea in the circumstances.

"What are we going to do if we see anybody?" I whispered.

LIGHTNING

"Nothing, man. We'll check out as much of this place as we can, then go back and tell the others what we found. Then we can make a plan."

"But we'll have to make ourselves known to the people here at some point," I said. "How are we going to get them to help us if we don't?"

He looked at me, the moonlight shining in his eyes. "Alex, you're really naïve, man. Do you think that some government scientists are going to help us, a bunch of civilians? They only look out for their own. They only gave the vaccine to the soldiers, not the general population. They won't give us anything. If there's a cure here, we're going to have to take it."

I wondered if I'd teamed up with a group of journalists or a sleeper cell of anarchists, poised to cause trouble for the government after the apocalypse hit. Sam, Tanya, and Jax seemed more capable than most when it came to survival and they were possessed of a certain kind of courage that was usually borne of a fundamental belief in something.

I told myself that was crazy. They had worked in some of the most dangerous places in the world and it had toughened them up, that was all. Still, taking over Survivor Radio and broadcasting a message to the listeners was the kind of operation usually carried out by people who had an agenda that went way beyond investigative journalism.

I hoped that their eagerness to find Apocalypse Island wasn't spurred on by some ulterior motive. If they did anything to jeopardize my chances of getting help for Lucy, I was going to flip my shit—and God help anyone who stood in my way.

I was out of breath by the time we reached the trees, but, looking back down the path, I realized how steep it was and how far we had climbed from the beach. I was in much better shape now than I had been when I was trudging over the Welsh mountains with Mike and Elena. If Mike could see me now, he'd be proud of how far I had come from the whiny, out of shape person I had once been. The zombie apocalypse was stripping me of pounds that I thought I was stuck with for life.

"Look at that, man," Sam said, pointing up into the trees. "I guess staying hidden isn't an option."

A small silver camera with a flashing red light above its lens watched us from high up in the branches of a pine tree. I was willing to bet we had already walked past a dozen more that we hadn't seen.

I waved at it.

Sam frowned at me. "Hey, what are you doing?"

"Like you said, staying hidden isn't an option anymore," I said. "And we want them to know we're friendly. If they're going to help us..."

"Trust no one, man. I thought you said you hated the authorities?"

"I do. But what choice do I have?"

He set off into the woods, following a dirt trail that wound through the trees. "Stop waving at the cameras."

I followed him through the dark woods. The sound of our boots crunching over dead leaves and fallen twigs on the road seemed so loud that anyone on the island must be able to hear our approach.

Sam stopped suddenly, putting a hand on my chest to halt me in my tracks. "Did you see that?" he whispered.

My eyes scanned the gloom ahead. "No. What was it?"

"Something moved in the undergrowth up ahead. By the side of the road." He pointed to the area I had already been watching.

I shrugged. "You sure?"

He nodded, tightening his grip on the baseball bat. I did the same, wondering why, if our own footsteps were so loud, we hadn't heard anyone walking in the undergrowth ahead of us.

Maybe they weren't walking. Maybe they were just waiting for us.

"What do we do?" I whispered.

Sam crept forward, gesturing for me to follow. I moved forward as quietly as I could, staying close behind him. Sam had a much better chance against whatever was in those trees than I did.

As we got closer, I saw a movement in the undergrowth, and nearly jumped out of my skin. I calmed my ragged breathing when I realized it was something small, maybe a squirrel or a bird.

But apart from the gulls we had seen on the other side of the island, I hadn't seen or heard a single bird since setting foot on the dock. In fact, now that I thought about it, the woods were eerily quiet, apart from the sounds we were making.

Sam strode up to the undergrowth and peered into it.

I heard a low moan that I knew all too well. The wail of a zombie.

"Get back!" I shouted.

"No, it's fine. It's just a head."

I went over and looked at the head lying on the ground. Its skin was the familiar mottled blue of the zombie, its eyes yellow as they glared at us. It opened its mouth and moaned again when it saw me.

The zombie had once been a man with a neat, short haircut, wearing a blue shirt beneath a white lab coat. But something had shredded the coat, shirt, and the rotten flesh beneath. The zombie had a head, neck, and part of his chest, but that was it. The arms had been ripped off, leaving a bloody mess where the shoulders had once been. Entrails lay on the ground like dead snakes.

"What do you think happened to him?" I asked Sam.

"I don't know, man. Either he got torn to pieces and then turned, or he was already a zombie before he got eaten or something."

My head snapped up when I heard another sound. Something was coming this way, running through the undergrowth toward us.

"What the fuck?" Sam whispered.

# LIGHTNING

"We need to get out of here," I said. I could see the figure crashing through the woods. He wore a dark blue security guard's uniform, complete with a baseball cap sporting the logo of whichever security firm he had worked for, and a black gun belt with a holstered sidearm. The veins in his neck and face were dark blue, spreading beneath the skin like a network of tentacles.

A hybrid. There was no way I could outrun him. Sam seemed unsure whether to run or fight, his hands flexing around the bat.

"The trees," I said. "I don't think they can climb." My limited experience with hybrids suggested they couldn't perform many actions beyond running and eating, but I was no expert when it came to monsters.

Sam nodded, and we began climbing the nearest pine. I had never been a tree climber, even when I was a kid, and the unwieldy baseball bat made the task even more difficult. Sam went up the tree like a big, loose-limbed monkey, and was out of the hybrid's reach in seconds.

My slow pace wasn't getting me out of danger quickly enough, and when the hybrid reached the tree, it reached up and grabbed my boot, pulling down with tremendous force.

Sam began to come down the tree to save me. "Hang on, man."

Hanging on was precisely what I was doing. My hands gripped the branch above my head so tightly that my fingers went numb. The hybrid was yanking at my boot as

15

if trying to pluck an apple from the tree. Its yellow eyes stared up at me, its face contorted by a mixture of determination and anger. I could see blue flesh hanging from its teeth, and I knew what had happened to the zombie on the ground; this hybrid had eaten it.

I couldn't hold on much longer. My body felt like it was being stretched on a medieval torture rack. My grip slipped, and I hit the ground so hard that it knocked the wind out of me. As I struggled for a breath that I knew would be my last, I tried to claw my way backward out of reach of the monster.

He came forward, moving quickly and preparing to claim the plump morsel he had pulled from the tree.

Sam was still too high in the branches to do anything to help me. I looked up at him, hoping he would do something to save me, but his attention was elsewhere, and he was staring at something behind me. Maybe the hybrid had a friend who wanted to feast on me too, and Sam was unable to look away, like the people who rubbernecked as they drove past a gory car crash.

Then I saw three red laser dots dance across the front of the blue uniform. The sound of automatic fire cracked through the air, and the hybrid fell to the ground.

I sat up and looked over my shoulder. Six men wearing identical security guard outfits as the hybrid had been wearing advanced to my position, assault rifles raised, red laser sights bouncing off the trees. They took up firing

LIGHTNING

positions on the road, aiming their weapons into the woods.

A seventh man strode up to me and stood with his hands on his hips. He had a military buzz cut and wore trousers patterned with woodland camouflage. A dark blue T-shirt clung tightly to his heavily muscled upper body.

"Gentlemen," he said in a rough voice, "come with me if you want to live."

# CHAPTER 3

HEY LED US ALONG THE road to where three dark-green Jeeps were parked. The man and his colleagues were silent as they led us to the vehicles. They bundled us into the back seat of a Jeep. Buzz Cut got into the front passenger seat, while one of his men drove us along the road.

"Right," Buzz Cut said, turning to look at us. "Let's get some names. Who are you?"

"I'm Alex, and this is Sam," I replied. Sam gave me a sideways glance that told me he didn't want me to give away any information, but I didn't see any point in being quiet now. These men were obviously connected with the island so maybe they could help us get to the person we needed to see regarding a cure. If there even is a cure, I reminded myself.

"My name is Ian Hart," Buzz Cut said. "I'm in charge of security on this island. Perhaps you'd like to tell me what you're doing here."

"We need help," I said. "Our friend has been bitten. I want to talk to the scientists here to see if they can help her."

He frowned. "There's no help for people who get bitten, son. They die. Then they come back as zombies. Then we shoot them. Game over."

I shook my head. "No, it's not that simple. My friend took the vaccine. She's still alive."

Hart raised an eyebrow. "How did she get the vaccine? Is she military personnel?"

"No, we got our hands on some," I said. "We've all been vaccinated."

He turned around in his seat to look out at the road and said nothing else.

The road broke through the trees and continued through flat grassland. In the distance, a square-shaped five-story building with rows of tinted windows came into view. A high, wire fence surrounded it, and the place looked like a typically nondescript government facility, complete with a parking lot out front where a few Jeeps were parked. I could see two military Chinook helicopters in a field by the side of the building, sitting next to a large hangar.

We drove up to a large gate, which was opened by a security guard in a sentry hut, and then through into the compound.

The driver parked the Jeep with the others, and Hart motioned for us to get out. We were led up to a set of glass doors. Hart swiped a card through a digital lock, and the doors opened into a reception area, which was deserted.

"Rooms five and six," he said to two of the men. They took us through a set of heavy doors and down a set of concrete steps to a white-painted corridor with doors lining the walls on each side. I was taken through one of them and left alone in the room, the guard shutting and locking the door after I was inside.

The room was unfurnished except for a metal table that was bolted to the floor and two wooden chairs. A large mirror was built into one wall, probably made of one-way glass like they had in police interview rooms. A camera was set high in the corner of the room, its red light blinking as it watched me.

I couldn't believe they were locking us up. Every second I was in this room was another second wasted in my attempt to save Lucy.

I slammed my palm on the table in frustration.

"Hey!" I shouted at the camera, "I need to speak to someone. You can't just leave me in here."

LIGHTNING

They *could* leave me in here, of course; they had guns and I was trespassing on their secret island. I supposed it would be ironic if I managed to survive against zombies and hybrids only to end up being murdered by security guards working for the government.

I paced the room, feeling helpless. I should have known not to trust the authorities. Sam had been right when he'd said to trust no one. Now, everything was fucked up. Lucy was going to become a hybrid in a few days time and I would probably still be rotting in this room.

It was a long time later when the door finally opened and Hart walked into the room. He held a brown folder under his arm, which he placed on the table before sitting down in one of the chairs.

"Take a seat, Alex," he said, motioning to the chair across the table from him.

I sat down and leaned across the table toward him. "Listen, my friend needs your help. If you want to lock me up, fine, but please help my friend. She doesn't have much time."

He looked at me coldly. "I'm going to ask you some questions, Alex. If you answer me truthfully, and I'm satisfied with your answers, then we can talk about helping your friend." He flicked through a pile of papers in the folder and took a pen from his pocket.

"I haven't got time for this bullshit," I said, slamming my hand down on the table again.

21

"If you want to help Lucy, you'll do exactly as I say." He positioned his pen over a blank piece of paper.

I frowned. "How do you know her name?"

"Your other friends told me." He consulted his notes. "Sam, Tanya, Jax, and Johnny. They're all here. My men brought them from your boat. We've been watching you on our cameras since you got within five miles of the island. Lucy is here, too, in a locked room on our hospital wing."

"You can help her," I said. "You have some kind of antidote, don't you? You can give it to her. Please, I…"

He held up a hand, silencing me. "Yes, there is an antidote, but it's not as simple as you seem to think it is. You saw those zombies out in the woods. The virus has hit us hard here and this facility isn't running at full strength. Now, do you want a chance to help Lucy or not?"

I nodded.

"Good. So tell me something; how have you survived for so long without being placed in a Survivors Camp, or being eaten by zombies? I know all about your Survivor Radio escapade; the others have told me about that. How did you stay alive before you met up with them?"

I told him about the hiking trip to Wales, about Mike and Elena, and our struggle to survive. I told him about my brother Joe and my parents being held somewhere in a Survivors Camp on the mainland. I recounted my journey to the coast with Lucy, Mike, and Elena. When I got to the

LIGHTNING

part about Mike's and Elena's deaths, I had to pause several times to keep my emotions in check; the loss of my best friend still hurt.

Hart listened and took notes. He showed no sign of any emotion himself, or even any reaction to my story other than a nod here and there as I told my tale.

When I got to the part where I had met Tanya, Sam, and Jax, he closed the folder. "Yes, I know the rest. Your friends speak highly of your actions. You're a survivor, Alex. You're resourceful and smart. You should be proud of how far you've come in these troubling times."

I said nothing. Flattery wasn't going to get him anywhere. All I wanted was a cure for Lucy. He'd said that it existed, and that was all I could focus on. I had that thin thread of hope to hang on to again.

"I can help Lucy," he said. "But I need something in return."

I nodded. "Name it."

"I need you to retrieve something for me from the mainland."

I said nothing. Suddenly, his condition for helping Lucy sounded like a suicide mission.

"As I mentioned before," he said, "we've been affected by the virus here. This facility is officially referred to as Site Alpha One, by the way—not 'Apocalypse Island' as the media liked to call us—and was once a successful scientific research site. I'm only the head of security, of course, so even I don't know everything that goes on here,

23

but the scientists who work here are all leaders in their fields. There are only a handful of those scientists left now.

"The virus that created the zombies began at Site Alpha Two, our sister site on the mainland. It spread from there to the general population and also to this island. We had staff moving back and forth between the sites, so it was inevitable the virus would find its way here.

"The interior of this building is clear now, but we have a few zombies and hybrids in the woods. The vaccine that was given to the army, the one that you and your friends have taken, was developed at Alpha Two. We were all injected with it, and then our hybrid problem began. Personnel started wandering off into the woods, wanting to be left alone. They were changing into hybrids, of course. That's what the virus does to people who have been vaccinated."

"I know," I said.

He grinned, but it was humorless. "Yes, of course you do. So here's the problem, Alex. The scientists here can manufacture an antivirus that halts the process of hybridization. Give it to someone who is turning into a hybrid, and it stops the process completely. It inhibits the reaction between the virus and the vaccine or it makes the vaccine stronger or something. I'm no scientist, so I can't give you all the chemical data. Not that you'd understand it anyway."

"You said there was a problem?" I said, wanting him to get to the point.

"Hmm, yes." He nodded. "The problem is that there's a chemical they need in order to manufacture the antivirus, called H1NZ1. It's something they synthesized at Alpha Two. We had a supply here, but there was an incident in one of our labs and the supply was destroyed. This was before the building was clear of zombies. One of our scientists tried to protect himself from an attack and ended up setting fire to the lab he was in. Bloody idiot. The entire lab was burned out, and with it, all of our H1NZ1.

"So there's no way we can make any of the antivirus that Lucy needs until we have more of that chemical."

He sat back in his chair, waiting for my answer.

What choice did I have? If I didn't do what he wanted, Lucy would turn. I would do anything to prevent that, even if it meant going to the mainland.

"I'll get it for you," I said.

# CHAPTER 4

GHOST OF A SMILE flickered across Hart's lips. "I knew you'd agree, Alex."

Something about the situation didn't make sense; he had armed and trained employees, so why was he asking me to go and get the chemical they needed? "If you need this chemical so badly, why haven't you sent your own people to get it?" I asked.

The smile disappeared from his face and he leaned forward, lowering his voice. "I'm not in charge here, Alex. The director of this facility has decided that obtaining the $H1NZ1$ isn't a priority for us. She's more focused on other things like clearing the island, and rebuilding our labs. There's a lot of damage to clean up from when we had zombies in here. We were fighting them in the building and a lot of the labs were destroyed in the process.

"So until this site is fully functional, the director isn't interested in anything else. She told me only this afternoon that it's too early for us to even think of salvaging materials from Site Alpha Two."

"Salvaging?" I asked. "You make it sound like Alpha Two is in ruins."

He shook his head. "No, not in ruins. Well, not physically anyway. We flew over there in our helicopters last week to take a look. The fences were still intact, the building still standing. But what it's like inside is anyone's guess. They had a zombie problem, same as us.

"After the zombie outbreak, both this site and Alpha Two were working on a vaccine against the zombies. We had scientists working in labs while my teams were fighting zombies in the corridors right outside the doors. The same kind of thing was happening at Alpha Two. It wasn't an ideal situation. Using video links and email, the scientists from here and Alpha Two worked together to develop the vaccine that was passed out to the soldiers on the mainland, the vaccine that we now know is faulty and creates hybrids

"Everyone here and at Alpha Two was also vaccinated, so the zombie problem at both sites eventually became a zombie and hybrid problem. The scientists continued working together to try and find a solution to the whole mess but then Alpha Two went offline. We lost all contact with them. After that, the scientists here came up with an antivirus that halts the process of hybridization but a key ingredient is H1NZ1. And all the H1NZ1 is at Alpha Two. So until we get our hands on it, there won't be any antivirus."

I looked at him closely, wondering if there was something he wasn't telling me. "If this H1 thing is so important, then I don't understand why you don't just go and get it yourself. You said you flew over the site in your helicopter. Why didn't you land and have a look around?"

"Like I told you, it wasn't a priority." He looked down at his notes but I could tell he wasn't really reading them; he was just trying to avoid looking me in the eye.

"No, there's more to it than that. Are you scared of something in that building?"

He sighed, but said nothing.

"If I'm going to go in there and get this chemical, I need to know what I'm going to be facing," I said.

He nodded. "Yes, I suppose you do. As I said, there was a zombie and hybrid problem both here and at Alpha Two. But Alpha Two had an additional problem. There was a monster at their site that was more dangerous than any normal hybrid. It was faster, even more savage in its attacks, and it possessed an intelligence and cunning that the zombies and hybrids don't have. We think it's because of this creature that Alpha Two went offline. And it's because of this creature that we don't think there's anyone left alive at that site."

LIGHTNING

I frowned, confused. How could there something worse than the hybrids? "I don't understand," I said. "How can there be a creature like that?"

"We aren't exactly sure. The people at Alpha Two weren't forthcoming with that information."

"Do you think it's something they created in their labs?" I asked him. "Some sort of experiment gone wrong?"

"No," he said, shaking his head grimly. "We think it's patient zero."

# CHAPTER 5

TELL ME WHAT HAPPENED," I said.

Hart shrugged. "We aren't exactly sure. We do know that the zombie outbreak began on the mainland in a town where some of Alpha Two's scientists lived among the general population. There was a cover up, and after a while the government thought everything was under control. But strange things began happening at Alpha Two. Personnel went missing. We heard rumors of a creature that was fast and deadly. This was before the vaccine had been developed. So there were no such things as hybrids then.

"The scientists were cagey about it but we surmised that the creature at their site was patient zero. It was the only thing that made sense. Again, I don't know all the scientific terms but apparently, patient zero could be very different from the zombies it created. The point is," he

# LIGHTNING

said, "Something deadly is still inside the building at Site Alpha Two. That's on top of all the hybrids and zombies that will be in there. Getting the H1NZ1 isn't going to be easy."

I nodded. Now it made sense why Hart and his team didn't go into the building after their flyover last week. "You said you were talking to the director this afternoon about salvaging the chemical. If you weren't going to risk going in there last week, why were you asking the director about it again today?"

He took a deep breath and let it out slowly between his lips before he answered. "Getting that chemical became a lot more important to me today than it was last week." He trailed off, seemingly lost in his thoughts.

"Why?" I prompted.

"My wife Kate is a lab technician here. That's how we met twelve years ago. She's all I have in this world, and I don't know what I'd do if anything happened to her. Today, at lunchtime, Kate and a few other people from the lab went beyond the fence to visit the beach by the dock. That probably sounds crazy to you, knowing what's out there on the island, but when you're cooped up in this compound day after day, you need a change of scenery or you'll go crazy. They took a Jeep and they had an armed guard with them."

He paused as if he didn't want to say next part. "They were attacked by a hybrid. Four people, including the guard, were killed. Kate was the only survivor. She drove the Jeep back here and demanded that she be put into quarantine immediately. She'd been bitten. She had the presence of mind to race back here before the virus sent her wandering away to find a quiet place to turn into a hybrid. So she's in our hospital right now, four days away from becoming a monster."

Now it all made sense. Hart needed the H1NZ1 bringing here just as much as I did. Without it, his wife would turn into a hybrid, the same as Lucy.

"So why don't you go and get it?" I asked. "You have trained people with weapons. If anyone has a chance to get the chemical from Alpha Two, it must be you and your team."

"Yes," he said, "but I can't go. The director won't bend her orders for me. She told me that if I left the island to get the H1, I wouldn't be allowed back. There are a lot of people here who would step into my position as soon as I left and enforce the director's orders. So even if I got the chemical, it wouldn't do Kate any good."

"But your director is okay with sending me," I said.

"You and your friends," he replied. "You aren't employees here, so as far as the director is concerned, if you get the H1 and bring it back here, then that's a bonus that she hasn't had to risk her own staff for. If you get killed and don't return, she won't have lost any of the island's resources. She has nothing to lose."

"So we're expendable," I said.

"To her you are," Hart said. "To me, you're the only people who can save my wife. That's why I'm going to give you all the weapons and equipment you need to succeed at this mission. You're my only hope, Alex."

I thought about it for a moment. "I'll do whatever it takes to save Lucy. But my friends don't even know her; I can't see them agreeing to go on this mission. Why would they?"

"Here's the situation, Alex. I can't send you alone to Site Alpha Two; you wouldn't stand a chance on your own. And as you say, if I let your friends go with you, I can't guarantee that they'll come back with the H1. If the mission got too tough, they might just abandon it. That would leave you and me in the shit where Kate and Lucy are concerned. I can't take that chance."

"So what are you going to do to make sure they return?" I asked, thinking I already knew the answer. He was going to keep one of us here, so that the others had to come back to collect them. Hart had probably guessed that we were a tight knit group and wouldn't abandon each other. "If you keep someone here," I said, "you'll reduce the number of people going on the mission by one, and also reduce our chance of success."

"No, nothing like that," he said. "I'm not going to keep any of you hostage. You'll all be going to Site Alpha Two. And I can guarantee that you will do everything you can to get the chemical and return." He stood up, went to the door, and knocked once.

A middle-aged man in a white lab coat entered. In his hands, he held a syringe filled with a pale blue liquid.

"Before you go to the mainland," Hart said, "we're going to inject you with the virus. You and your friends have all been vaccinated, so it won't kill you and bring you back as zombies. You'll have four days before you turn into hybrids, the same as Kate and Lucy. The only way you can stop that from happening is by bringing the H1NZ1 here so we can make the antivirus to stop the change."

The guy in the lab coat removed the plastic cap that protected the syringe's needle.

"Wait a minute," I said. "You've seen what happens to people who are changing into hybrids. They get sick and helpless. We can't get the chemical if we're like that."

The scientist nodded. "That's what happens when a vaccinated person gets bitten by a zombie. This is different." He held up the syringe. "It's a pure strain of the virus that doesn't react violently with the vaccine in your system. You won't get sick. The change will be gradual. It won't make you ill until the fourth day."

"So you'll have three days to get the H1NZ1, and get back here," Hart added.

"But you know I'll come back," I protested. "I won't leave Lucy. You don't need to inject me with anything."

Hart shrugged. "Well if you're planning to come back anyway, then what's the difference?"

LIGHTNING

"Have the others agreed to this?" I asked. I'd always hated needles but knowing that this one contained the virus that turned people into monsters made me fear it.

Hart laughed mirthlessly. "Of course not. They didn't have a choice. I had to have them held down while they were injected. I was hoping that, given your circumstances, that wouldn't be necessary with you."

I had no choice. If I didn't agree to be injected, they'd force it on me anyway. And like Hart said, I was planning on coming back here with the H1NZ1, so what was the difference? I looked at the scientist. "Do it."

He came forward, lifted the sleeve of my T-shirt, and pushed the needle into my shoulder muscle. I winced and drew in a sharp breath. He pressed the plunger on the syringe, and I felt a stinging sensation spread through my arm.

When he was done, the scientist left the room.

"Good," Hart said, smiling. "Now, time is of the essence. So, let's go and meet your friends and plan how we're going to get that chemical."

"No," I said. "I want to see Lucy first."

He gave me a thin-lipped smile. "Of course."

\*\*\*

The facility's hospital was modern and well equipped. Like all hospitals, the wards smelled of disinfectant, and there was a constant bleeping from various machines that were hooked up to patients.

Hart led me past the main ward to a small corridor where the doors were all closed and, I assumed, locked. He pointed to a window. I looked through it to see Lucy lying in a hospital bed. She was lying, curled up, beneath the sheets. There were no machines attached to her, no drips, and no tubes. None of those things would do her any good. The only thing that could save her now was the antivirus.

Hart was looking into the window of the room next to Lucy's. There was a woman in there lying in exactly the same curled-up position as Lucy.

"My wife, Kate," Hart said.

I nodded.

"I'm relying on you, Alex," he said.

"Don't worry. I'll get that chemical."

"Okay. Now, let's go and discuss that with the others. We need to get started as soon as possible."

I followed him along the corridor. I didn't want to leave Lucy here but I was acutely aware that I had a ticking time bomb running through my veins that had to be defused.

If I didn't get the H1NZ1 back here from the mainland in time, that bomb was going to blow, and it would mean the end of everything.

# CHAPTER 6

THE OTHERS WERE WAITING IN a large lecture hall, all of them sitting on the front row of seats like the most attentive students in the world. The fact that we all had the virus in our systems was definitely motivating; Hart had been right about that. I took a seat next to Johnny. He turned to me with an accusing look in his dark eyes. Tanya, Sam, and Jax just ignored me.

They probably blamed me for the situation we found ourselves in, but I hadn't forced them to come to Apocalypse Island. In fact, I'd told them I should come alone, so I refused to be held responsible for any of this.

Hart took the stage, and as he did so, the lights in the room dimmed. A large screen came to life, displaying a photograph of a building identical to the one we were in now, except that the five-story building on the screen was located in a fenced-in compound, and beyond the fence, rolling green hills were visible.

"This is Site Alpha Two," Hart said. Unlike Alpha One, where we are now, Alpha Two is on the mainland. It's in a remote area of the Scottish highlands. A fifteen-foot-high fence protects the facility, with razor wire running along the top. The security there was high level, as it is here.

"When we flew over the site a week ago, we ascertained that the fence had been compromised in some places, and that there were no signs of life inside the compound."

The screen changed, showing a blueprint of corridors and rooms. "This is the fourth floor of the building. The lab at the end of this corridor is where you are most likely to find the H1NZ1. This is where the chemical was synthesized. There may also be a supply of the chemical in the storeroom here." He pointed to a different room on the blueprint. "We'll provide you with maps of every floor, as well as weapons. We want you to have the best chance possible of retrieving the H1NZ1 and bringing it to the rendezvous point."

The screen showed an overhead satellite image of the area, Site Alpha Two no more than a small box on the terrain. "This area here," Hart said, indicating a point that looked like it was a couple of miles from the building, "is where we'll land the chopper to drop you off. We can't land any closer to the building, because the noise of the helicopter will attract all the zombies from miles around. You'll have enough to deal with inside the building; there's no point attracting more to the area. So you'll exit the chopper here, and remove yourselves from the location quickly.

"When we pick you up, we'll use this helipad to the north of the facility. It was used to transport staff from one site to another. We can't wait for long in the pick-up area because the noise of the helicopter will bring all the zombies our way. We'll be there at 1300 hours on Tuesday. Today is Sunday, so that will give you plenty of time to locate the chemical and get back to the rendezvous point, and also means that you'll get back here long before the virus in your blood has a chance to do anything to you. The noise of the helicopter will bring any zombies in the area our way, so when I say 1300 hours, I don't mean 1305, or even 1302. Be there on time for all our sakes."

The screen went black and the lights in the room came up. A scientist with dark hair and glasses came down from the back of the room and ascended the steps to the stage.

He said, "My name is Doctor Gorman. The H1NZ1 you're looking for will be held in glass vials, which are kept in small metallic boxes about the size of a deck of playing cards. The designation H1NZ1 will be stenciled on the boxes. Bring back as many as you can. The vials are encased in foam rubber within the metal boxes, so don't worry about them breaking if you have to handle them roughly."

"Any questions?" Hart asked.

"This is bullshit, man," Sam muttered.

"That's not a question, it's a statement," Hart said. "Any questions?"

"How do we get to the fourth floor?" Tanya asked. "There must be security doors with digital locks just like there are at this site."

Gorman spoke up. "We'll provide you with access cards for the entire facility. They will open every door. The electricity on the mainland is still working thanks to the army, so the digital locks will all be functional."

"Anything else?" Hart asked.

"Yeah," Johnny said. "After we get back here, how long does it take to make the antivirus that's going to cure us?"

"It will take an hour to produce it once we have the H1NZ1," Gorman said.

"Let's go, man," Sam said, standing up. "I want to get this shit over with." He started for the door at the back of the room.

Hart nodded. "The chopper is waiting. We have a selection of weapons for you to choose from in the hangar."

# CHAPTER 7

HE WEAPONS WERE LAID OUT on a wooden table in one of the hangars. There was also a third Chinook in here, this one being worked on by a team of mechanics. The hangar smelled of burnt metal and oil.

I looked at the array of weapons on offer and felt overwhelmed by choices. There were handguns, rifles, machine guns, boxes of ammo, knives, baseball bats, and axes. There were also five backpacks so we could carry the H1NZ1 boxes and still use our weapons.

"Awesome," Sam said, picking up an assault rifle that I recognized from various video games as a Heckler & Koch MP5.

"Is that a wise choice?" I asked Sam. "If you fire that thing, you'll attract every nasty in the area."

"Fuck you, Alex. I'm taking it." He began loading ammo into one of the backpacks. Then, maybe because he realized I was right about the noise the gun would make, he also took a baseball bat.

Since being injected with the virus, Sam's attitude toward me had gone from friendly to aggressive. I wanted to tell him that none of us were happy with the situation, that we had to make the best of it, but I didn't think talking to him was a good idea right now. Let him take time to come to terms with what had happened to us. Maybe he would realize it wasn't my fault.

"Don't forget water and rations," Hart said, pointing to another table that held survival gear. As well as canteens of water and military ration packs, there were glow sticks, flashlights, waterproof matches, lengths of para cord, and five sets of folded papers sealed in clear plastic bags. I assumed these were the maps of Site Alpha Two. The door cards were in the same bags.

I picked up a baseball bat from the table and also selected a handgun. The gun was in a leather holster, which I attached to my belt.

"Jesus," Sam muttered. "He tells me not to bring a gun, and then he chooses a Desert Eagle."

"That's loaded with eight .44 rounds," Hart said. "Will you need any extra cartridges?"

I shook my head. I was only planning on using the gun in the direst of circumstances because of the noise issue I had mentioned to Sam. One of those circumstances would be if the nasties cornered me. In that case, one of those eight bullets had my name on it.

## LIGHTNING

Pushing that thought from my mind, I loaded water and rations into my backpack, along with a handful of glow sticks, matches, a flashlight, and a length of para cord. I had no idea if all of that was going to come in handy, but I didn't want to find myself in a situation later where I wished I had something that I hadn't bothered to bring along.

Johnny also took a pistol and a bat. When I saw the worried look on his face, I wondered if he regretted leaving the Survivor Radio studios to join us. He might have been a prisoner there, but at least he never had to risk his life by going into a huge facility that was probably full of zombies.

Tanya took a bat and an MP5, shooting me a rebellious look as she picked up the assault rifle. Okay, I got the idea; for some reason I was being held responsible for everything and everyone was mad at me. I turned away from Tanya's gaze and watched the mechanics working on the Chinook. I was used to being the outsider, the person everyone in a group thought was weird, and avoided. But I thought that a bond of friendship had been forged between Tanya, Jax, Sam, and myself. We had been through a lot together.

And it was all very well for Tanya to be picking up an assault rifle and shooting me a dirt look but I was still right about the use of guns in the building. If we went in there all guns blazing, we wouldn't last more than a few seconds. Every zombie and hybrid in the place would know our location, and it was only a matter of time before we ran out of bullets.

Jax took a bat, a knife, and a Desert Eagle. She attached the knife and sidearm to her belt and then went to the other table to load her backpack with survival gear.

Hart stood watching us with a grim expression on his face. We were the only chance he had of curing his wife, and he was probably thinking that the probability of us returning alive, and with the H1NZ1, was very low.

"Is everyone ready?" he asked when we had all slung our backpacks over our shoulders.

We nodded like a group of condemned prisoners about to face a firing squad.

"Let's go," Hart said. He led us out of the hangar and across the asphalt, beneath the night sky, to the Chinook. He waved to the pilot, and the engines began to hum, the twin rotor blades spinning lazily at first, and then picking up speed until they chopped the air with the familiar droning sound that gave helicopters their nickname.

The rear ramp descended, and we walked up it and into the cylindrical interior of the Chinook. A row of pull-down seats made of red canvas and metal poles lined the walls. I sat down and stowed my backpack by my feet. The helicopter was huge, allowing everyone to sit some distance from their neighbor, each of us lost in our own thoughts. Hart sat across from me, his eyes sad and weary. He probably didn't hold much hope of our group returning alive with the chemical needed to save his wife.

# LIGHTNING

I was wondering if I was ever going to see Lucy again. If this mission went badly, and I died at Site Alpha Two, she would turn into a hybrid, and be killed. I would have failed her.

Never in my life had I been so responsible for someone. Before everything had turned to shit, I had forced myself to go to my dead-end job during the week and spent the weekends zoning out on video games. The most responsibility I'd had was to my teammates during online-gaming sessions. At that time, Lucy Hoffmeister had been nothing more than a faraway dream, a fantasy.

Now, I held her life in my hands. The old Alex would have balked at such a thing, preferring to lose himself in a world that wasn't real. Now, the real world had hit me square in the face, and it had changed me forever.

The Chinook lifted straight up into the air, making my stomach lurch. Then we flew over the sea toward the mainland, leaving Apocalypse Island behind.

# CHAPTER 8

W E DESCENDED AFTER A SILENT, thirty-minute flight. It was noisy inside the belly of the Chinook, but nobody even tried to make conversation over the constant hum of the engines. Tanya sat studying her maps while the rest of us simply sat staring at the walls.

When we touched down, the rear of the helicopter opened, revealing a grassy field beneath the stars. The night was clear and dry, the moon bright and almost full, splashing the field with silver moonlight. It was a good night for zombies.

"Come on, people," Hart said, "let's move." He made sweeping motions with his hands, ushering us off the chopper and out into the night. As I was about to step onto the ramp, he grabbed my shoulder and looked into my eyes earnestly. "See you in a couple of days, Alex. Don't let Kate and Lucy down."

LIGHTNING

"I won't," I said, sounding more confident than I felt.

He nodded, and then disappeared back into the helicopter. I walked down the ramp and into the long grass.

"We need to leave this area now," Tanya said, adjusting her backpack before marching away across the field toward a low stone wall.

We all followed, advancing across the field toward the wall as the Chinook lifted into the air, its rotors flattening the long grass behind us. Hart had been right about the noise; if there were zombies in the area, they were sure to hear the chopper and come this way.

We seemed to be in a farmer's field. The farmhouse sat in darkness a couple of miles away, and the night breeze smelled of cows. I couldn't see any in this field or the next, but we passed an open gate in the wall, so the cattle might have wandered off, leaving only their smell behind.

Tanya stopped and took out a map from her pocket. "The compound is a few miles beyond the farm," she said, pointing at a low, dark hill in the distance. "Over there." She turned to look at us all. "Do we go tonight, or wait until morning?"

"Let's do it, man," Sam said. "The sooner we finish this bullshit task, the better."

"I'm with Sam," Johnny said. "We should get this over with."

"I'm not so sure that's a good idea." I pointed at the farmhouse. "Maybe we should hole up in there for the

47

night and go to the facility in the morning. It's already late, and we'll be getting tired soon. I'd rather spend the night in that farmhouse than in the labs."

"I'm not tired at all," Sam said. "I'm ready to kick ass. For some reason, I feel a sense of urgency. Oh, wait, maybe it's because I have the fucking zombie virus in my blood." He looked at me sharply.

"I didn't make you go to Apocalypse Island," I reminded him. "In fact, I said I'd go alone."

"If it wasn't for your stupid girlfriend getting herself bitten, we wouldn't be here at all," he said.

The emotions that had been simmering inside me all day boiled over, and I lashed out at Sam. My punch, which I had been aiming at his face, connected with his shoulder. He was fast, and even as I was withdrawing my fist for a second blow, he drove his own fist into my stomach, forcing the air out of my lungs in an explosive whoosh. I fell down and lay in the grass, clutching my belly and trying to breathe.

Sam stood over me. "If anybody gets killed on this mission, I'm blaming you, Alex. Their blood will be on your hands."

"Stop it," Tanya said, pulling him away. "You two can fight it out when we get back with the H1 stuff, and we've all been given the antivirus. Until then, we need to work together or none of us will be going back alive."

Sam glared at her but seemed to take her words on board. He backed away and sat on the stone wall, sulking.

LIGHTNING

I managed to suck in some breaths and stagger to my feet. I stood with my hands on my hips, looking up at the stars while I breathed slowly and tried to ignore the pain in my stomach.

Jax put a hand on my shoulder. "Are you okay, Alex?"

I nodded.

Johnny pointed into the dark, at the place the helicopter had landed. "We should get moving."

I turned to see at least a dozen zombies shambling toward us. They were the slow-moving kind, trudging through the grass with hungry determination.

Tanya set off toward the farmhouse. "Come on."

Jax and I followed while Sam and Johnny sauntered behind us, muttering to each other.

"Are we going to the farmhouse?" I asked Tanya. She seemed to have assumed leadership of our group. We all knew how tough she was, and I couldn't think of a better person to take charge.

"No," she said, shaking her head. "We need to get to that chemical as quickly as possible, while we're still working together. If the group splits apart because of arguments, it's going to be a hell of a lot harder to complete this mission."

Her talk of the group splitting apart sounded like an overreaction to me. Sure, everyone was mad at me because they all thought it was my fault we were here, but I didn't think the group would split because of it. Or were everyone's emotions running hotter than I knew? Maybe the others had been talking about me behind my back.

I was beginning to feel like an outsider again, and I didn't like it. We had all been through a lot together, so why couldn't' we be friends? Maybe I was too naive; in the old world, the world before the living dead had appeared, people like Sam and Tanya would never be friends with someone like me. We were too different.

But I had assumed that in this new world, that could change because we all had something in common: we were survivors.

A shot cracked the air behind us. I whirled around to see Sam standing in a firing position with the MP5 braced against his shoulder. One of the zombies that had been following us collapsed to the ground.

"Head shot" Sam said proudly. "Right between the eyes."

"You idiot," I said. "You're going to bring every nasty in the area down on us."

"Shut up, man."

"Alex is right," Tanya said to Sam. "The more noise we make, the more trouble we're going to find ourselves in."

He shrugged, lowering the weapon.

I heard a sound like a bee buzzing past my face before a bullet slammed into the wall. The sound of a gunshot reached us seconds later

"Get down," I shouted.

LIGHTNING

A second bullet hit the wall, cracking into the rocks. I waited to hear the shot so I could gauge where it was coming from.

"It's coming from the house," Jax said when the sound reached us.

Muzzle flash appeared in an upstairs window. A bullet thudded into the ground somewhere near Tanya's face. We scrambled over the stone wall quickly. As I landed on the opposite side, I glanced over my shoulder. Some of the zombies, seeing us go over the wall, had shambled through the open gate so they were on the same side as us.

"Zombies heading this way," Johnny said.

We began to crawl beside the wall, away from the zombies. No more shots came from the farmhouse; whoever was in there shooting at us, was smart enough not to waste bullets when they couldn't see us.

A short distance ahead, a second wall bisected the wall we were following at a ninety-degree angle. If we tried to go over it, we would expose ourselves to the mystery shooter. If we stopped, the zombies would reach us.

We scrambled up against the second wall, putting our backs against it so that we faced the advancing horde.

Tanya readied her MP5. Sam began shooting. When Tanya was locked and loaded, she joined him in spraying bullets at the zombies. They went down easily enough when they were hit in the head, but I couldn't help wondering how many more were going to arrive when they heard all the noise the guns were making. Sam and Tanya were probably making a bad situation worse by tearing up the night with bullets.

After a brief burst of muzzle flash and ear cracking bangs from the assault rifles, the zombies on this side of the wall lay unmoving in the grass.

"What now?" Jax asked no one in particular.

We were pinned here. If we left the safety of the wall, we would become targets for the shooter in the farmhouse.

My peripheral vision caught a movement in the darkness. I turned to glance into the field we were sitting in, and my heart began hammering.

Three figures were running toward us. In the starlight, I could just make out the camouflage pattern of their army uniforms.

"We need to move," I said. "Hybrids."

# CHAPTER 9

SAM AND TANYA TURNED THEIR weapons on the hybrids, but as soon as they began firing, the hybrids dropped to the ground and came scuttling through the grass on all fours like spiders, presenting smaller targets. And they were crawling fast.

"We have to go over the wall," I said. "The only safe place around here is that house."

"There's a guy in there trying to kill us," Tanya reminded me.

"I'd rather face a human being with a gun than deal with...that," I said, nodding at the approaching hybrids.

"Yeah," she agreed. "Let's go. We're making a run for the farmhouse. Sam, lay down some cover fire."

Sam leaned over the wall and fired a few rounds at the upstairs window of the house. "Go!" he shouted.

We scrambled over the wall, and sprinted for the farmhouse. As we ran, Tanya brought up her rifle and let off a few shots toward the window we had been targeted from. I heard glass shatter, and a startled cry, and wondered if the shooter in the house had been hit by glass shards, if not by Tanya's bullet.

Sam caught up with us, breathing hard.

The farmhouse was built of stone, with double-glazed windows and a front door that looked like it was made of heavy wood. It wasn't going to be easy to get inside. We ran around the back, and as we reached the corner of the house, I risked a glance over my shoulder.

The three hybrids were back on their feet, sprinting toward us.

"We don't have much time," I said to Tanya. My words were rushed as I gasped for air. I wasn't built for running, but at least I had reached the farmhouse without stopping. There was once a time when I wouldn't have been able to make that run. I'd be lying in the grass back there while the hybrids tore into me and ripped me apart.

The back door looked less heavy duty than the front, but it still looked sturdy enough to withstand being forced open.

"Fuck," Sam said. "We can't go through there." He turned to face the advancing hybrids, the assault rifle raised so he could look along the sights.

Tanya aimed her rifle at the kitchen window and blew it to pieces, glass crashing everywhere. "Be careful," she said as she climbed through. Jax followed and then I climbed in, wary of the deadly looking pieces of glass lying on the kitchen counter on the other side of the window.

Johnny and Sam followed quickly.

"They'll follow us in here," I said.

"That won't matter," Tanya said. She and Sam pointed their guns at the space where the window had once been. "They'll have to come through that gap, and when they do, we'll blast them."

The first hybrid appeared, his yellow eyes filled with determination and hate. Both MP5s spat bullets, and the hybrid's head jerked back, crimson blood gushing from its face.

The second hybrid appeared, clambering past the window frame, driven by a sense of rage far stronger than any sense of self-preservation. After the MP5s spoke a second time, the hybrid's lifeless body slid heavily from the counter onto the kitchen floor and lay dead at our feet.

I wondered how strong the bloodlust must be in these monsters that it drove them to attack without any regard for their own lives.

A flurry of gunfire dispatched the third hybrid before it even managed to get through the broken window.

"Sam, find the stairs and cover them," Tanya said. "There's someone up there who wants us dead. The rest of you, help me move that table to cover the opening."

We wrestled with a heavy wooden table that had been sitting in one corner of the kitchen and positioned it over the hole where the window had once been. By sliding the refrigerator across the floor and pushing it up against the table's legs, we managed to press the table firmly in place, covering the gap.

There were still plenty of zombies out there, but we knew they didn't have the basic intelligence of the hybrids; zombies would walk past that table-covered opening and not even think about trying to break in.

"Any trouble, Sam?" Tanya shouted out.

"Nothing," he replied from somewhere in the house. "Whoever was shooting at us is holed up somewhere upstairs."

We left the kitchen and walked along a hallway to where Sam was crouched at the foot of a flight of stairs, MP5 aimed at the landing above.

I glanced through a door into a living room. The house was furnished simply in a rustic manner, but looked comfortable. You would never know from the quiet atmosphere in the house that a zombie apocalypse was sweeping across the land outside.

Through the window, I saw some of the zombies pass by the house, nothing more than dark shapes in the night. I knew they would roam around out there until something else caught their attention and drew them away. They functioned on a very basic level, their actions controlled by the virus that infected their dead bodies. Their simple, dead minds had no reasoning power.

# LIGHTNING

The people upstairs were another matter entirely. Armed, and presumably smart, they presented the greatest immediate danger to us.

I assumed there was more than one person up there, because the framed photographs on the mantelpiece in the living room showed a couple in their sixties, and whom I presumed to be two sons in their thirties.

That meant that there were potentially four armed people to deal with up there.

I told the others.

"Fuck 'em," Sam said. "We've probably got better firepower. I say we go up there and clear all the rooms."

I had to stop myself from rolling my eyes. When did we become a SWAT team? We were being sidetracked from what was important.

"Or we could just leave," I said. "I saw a set of car keys hanging on the wall near the back door. We can take their car and get to Site Alpha Two much quicker. We aren't here to murder people."

"They shot at us," Sam said.

"And who can blame them? They're probably scared shitless, trying to protect their farm from zombies. Wouldn't you shoot at trespassers if it was you?"

He shrugged. "I guess so."

"What kind of car is it?" Tanya asked.

"I don't know. The keys have the Volkswagen logo on them."

Jax went into the living room and peered out of the window. "I don't see any car out there, and there wasn't one at the front of the house, either."

I went back to the kitchen, grabbed the keys, and found a door that opened into a garage. It was neat, with tools hanging on the walls in ordered rows, a stack of tires in one corner, and a smell of oil and rubber in the air.

When I had first seen the VW keys, I had wondered if the car might be a Beetle, or something compact that we wouldn't all fit into. I needn't have worried; a metallic-blue Volkswagen California camper van sat in the garage.

The others appeared at the door.

Jax said, "Sweet."

"I'll drive," Tanya said. "We need to get the garage door open."

"It's automatic," I said. "There's a remote opener in the van."

Tanya climbed into the driver's seat, with Sam next to her up front. The rest of us piled into the spacious rear area. Tanya hit the button on the remote and the garage door slid slowly upward to reveal a gravel driveway beyond and a dirt road beyond that.

Tanya started the engine, turned on the headlights, and got the camper van into gear, revving the engine while she waited for the door to open enough to let the camper van through.

When we finally drove out of the garage and into the night, Tanya said, "Hang on," as something thumped off the side of the vehicle. She gunned the engine and we shot forward down the driveway, gravel crunching under the tires, and onto the narrow dirt road.

I could hear moans beyond the windows, but we quickly left the zombies behind as we drove away, the headlights illuminating the deserted road.

"Do you know the way?" Jax asked Tanya.

Tanya nodded. "I think so." She kept her eyes on the road ahead.

Sam turned to us, looking into the back of the van over his seat. "Did you see the way those hybrids hit the deck and came at us like spiders? That was some fucked-up shit, man."

"Yeah," I said. The hybrids scared me much more than the zombies. I remembered when I was reading zombie novels and playing zombie video games that there would always be a debate about shambling zombies versus running zombies. I always thought that running zombies were too dangerous. Now, I knew how true that was. The hybrids moved so fast that it would be easy to get caught by them. And they had an appetite for flesh, even rotting zombie flesh.

I thought back to how they had ignored the shambling zombies by the stone wall and come after us instead, even though we were running away. They obviously preferred their meals to be alive and kicking.

We turned off the main road—if the dirt track could be called a main road—and drove along a narrow track that cut through a wood. Dark trees rolled past my window, and I wondered how many zombies were in there among the pines. Woods inhabited by monsters were once just a thing of fairy tales, but longer. Now, the stories of flesh-eating monsters were true. And just like in the fairy tales, anyone wandering into the trees might never be seen again.

We bumped along the track for half an hour before emerging from the trees. Tanya hit the brakes and the camper van came to a stop in front of a tall wire fence topped with razor wire. Beyond the fence sat a five-story building identical to the one on Apocalypse Island. Although the second floor windows were all dark, the lights on the other floors were switched on, giving the impression that the building was full of people.

A small yellow sign on the fence had six black words stenciled onto it: Government property. Trespassers will be prosecuted.

"I can't see any people," Jax said, leaning forward in her seat. "But why are all the lights still on?"

"Nobody bothered to turn them off," I guessed. "When everybody is being eaten by zombies, saving energy isn't a priority."

"Let's not jump to conclusions," Tanya said. "For all we know, there might be another reason they lost contact with Alpha One. Maybe everybody in there is alive and well."

# LIGHTNING

I wasn't sure about that, and Tanya herself didn't sound convinced. There was an eerie, deathly-quiet atmosphere around Site Alpha Two.

"So what's the plan?" Sam asked.

"We don't have one." Tanya turned in her seat. "Anyone have any ideas?"

"I think we need to take it slow, and see what we're getting ourselves into before we go in there all guns blazing," I said.

"Typical," Sam said.

"So do you think the best idea is to go storming through the door and advertise our presence to everybody in there, zombie or otherwise?" I asked, annoyed that Sam seemed to be contradicting everything I said just for the hell of it. "Didn't Hart tell you about patient zero? Because he told me there's a creature in there that's worse than any hybrid. Do you want to go blundering into the building if that's waiting in there for you?"

"Of course not, man, but there's such a thing as too much caution. We can't go sneaking around forever. The chopper will be coming back for us the day after tomorrow. By then, we need to get to the fourth-floor labs, grab the H1 whatever, and get out again. We can't do all that by fucking about."

"All I'm saying is that we should try to get some idea of what we're stepping into," I said.

"We know what we're stepping into, man. It's called shit."

61

"I have an idea," Johnny said. I looked over at him. He had one of the maps of the facility open on his lap. "Look here," he said, pointing at a small structure located inside the fence but separate from the main building. "This is a security guard station. And according to this diagram, there are monitors in there. What if they monitor the security cameras in the main building? We could see what's going on in there before we walk in through the front door."

"Good idea," Tanya said. "Where is that building?"

Johnny studied the map and looked out of the camper van window to get his bearings. "If you follow the road around to the left, we should come to a main gate. This building is about fifty yards inside from there."

Tanya turned the steering wheel and took us along the road that ran around the perimeter of compound. I looked closely at Site Alpha Two as we followed the fence toward the main gate. There was no movement in there that I could see. If the place was full of zombies, they were waiting quietly inside.

But I knew that as soon as we entered the building, they wouldn't be quiet anymore.

# CHAPTER 10

E ARRIVED AT THE MAIN gate at the same time as a light drizzle began falling. I hadn't noticed that the sky, which had been clear earlier, was now murky. Even the moon, which had been so bright when the Chinook had dropped us off in the field, was partly obscured from our sight by dark clouds. Typical. Just as we were about to enter a dangerous area, the night got dark. It would make it much more difficult to see if there were zombies or hybrids wandering around inside the compound.

The gate was closed, but when Sam got out of the camper van and went to check if it was locked, it swung open. Sam waited while Tanya drove us inside before closing the gate again. When he got back into the vehicle, I asked him why had had closed it.

"We don't know what's in those woods, man. We don't want something following us in here."

I nodded. His argument was sound. On a quiet night like this, even the gentle idling noise made by the camper van's engine would drift through the trees, attracting whatever was in those woods. It might be a good idea to barricade the gate somehow, but then we could be locking ourselves in with a much worse monster than anything outside the compound.

The guard station was a single-story brick building with lighted windows, sitting across the parking lot from the main building. A few cars were parked in the lot, waiting for owners who would never return. The guard station had a single door, which had a glass panel set into it at eye level. Sam checked it out, peering through the glass before giving us the thumbs-up signal. "It's clear," he said, opening the door.

Tanya switched off the engine and sudden silence descended. That silence seemed to be laced with an anticipation of danger, as if something was going to come quietly out of the night and take us one by one, like an owl swooping noiselessly onto its prey, razor sharp claws bared.

I had to stop thinking like that or I was going to spook myself to the point that every tiny noise was going to make me jump.

We got out of the van and walked through the cold drizzle to the guard station.

LIGHTNING

It was warm inside the small building, the radiators on the wall throwing out more than enough heat to combat the chill of the night. There was a single main room, a restroom, and a storeroom that held a filing cabinet and a coffee machine.

The main room had a row of a six monitors affixed to one of the walls, each with a number 1-6 painted on the wall above it, with a row of desks and chairs beneath, each desk holding a small control panel. The monitors were switched on, displaying black and white images of the parking lot, the perimeter fence, and various corridors that I assumed were inside the main building. A row of walkie-talkies sat in a charger on one of the desks.

"The main building looks deserted," Jax said, watching the monitors.

It was true that the screens seemed to show an empty building, but they only showed corridors. The only room interiors shown were two small rooms that looked like the mirrored room I had been held in at Alpha One.

"There are only six monitors," I said. "That's a huge building, so these screens aren't showing everything in there. The guards must select which cameras to monitor using the control panels."

I took a seat at one of the desks and looked at the controls. There were two rows of white buttons beneath labels that denoted which camera they were related to. There was a small joystick that I assumed controlled the cameras' movements. There was also a button that said

*Audio* with an On and Off position. It was currently turned to off, and the button for the *Level 1 Main Corridor* was depressed. I clicked the button next to it, labeled *Level 5 Elevators*, and one of the screens changed the image to show three closed elevator doors and a section of corridor. The camera was obviously set high up on the wall opposite the elevators, the image looking down from that vantage point.

Something moved across the screen suddenly. A woman in a skirt and blouse came into view, walking along the corridor slowly, aimlessly. She wore thick-rimmed glasses that were broken, the right half of the frame hanging loosely, the lens missing. That didn't seem to bother her. She stared vacantly ahead as if in a trance. I couldn't see any wounds on her that would indicate that she'd been bitten but because the image was black and white, I had no idea if her flesh was mottled blue or if her eyes were the hateful yellow of the zombie. She passed from the view of the camera.

"What's up with her, man?" Sam asked.

"I don't know," I said.

Everyone took a seat and began hitting various buttons on the control panels, switching cameras until they found something of interest.

After a few minutes, each monitor showed a very different scene to the one it had displayed when we'd first entered the room.

I studied each monitor in turn. The second floor main corridor was blacked out. It looked like the power had been cut from that floor, although the cameras were still working so they must have been operating on a separate electrical circuit.

The fourth floor elevator camera showed the closed doors of the elevators and, lying in front of them, the bodies of four security guards, all lying face down and dressed in the same uniforms and caps as the guards at Alpha One. They were covered in blood and guts. A dark pool of blood had spread across the floor from where the bodies lay. Had they been killed by something that had ripped out their insides, or had they been gutted after death? They hadn't turned, suggesting a cause of death other than a zombie bite.

The first floor reception area seemed deserted. When we went through the main door into the building, this would be where we'd begin our journey to the fourth-floor labs. The camera showed a wide-open space, decorated with a few large potted plants and a seating area. The reception desk itself sat behind a semi-circular wooden counter. The camera also showed the three closed elevator doors. But unlike the fourth floor, there was no sign of carnage here.

I turned to the others. "At least our entry point into the building looks safe enough."

Tanya nodded. "Well, it's not crawling with nasties, anyway." She pointed to the monitor that showed the guards lying dead by the elevators on the fourth floor. "But what the hell happened to them?"

"I don't know," I said.

Sam said, "It looks like a straight forward snatch and grab to me, man. We go into the reception area, get an elevator up to the fourth floor, step over the bodies, and go down this corridor to the lab." He pointed to the next monitor, which showed the deserted fourth-floor corridor. The lab doors were all closed. If there were any nasties on that floor, they were hopefully sealed behind those doors. "Then we get the H1 stuff, ride the elevator back to the first floor, and get the fuck out of there. We spend the rest of tonight, and all of tomorrow, in the van. The day after that we drive to the pick-up point for one o' clock. It's so easy, it's almost like a vacation."

"It sounds too easy," Tanya said.

I didn't say anything, but I agreed with Tanya. I wanted this mission to be as easy as Sam had said, but I didn't dare hope that it would be. My hopes had been destroyed too many times in the past.

The other two monitors showed the facility's cafeteria, which had at least fifty zombies wandering between the tables, and the third-floor corridor, which was deserted. Unlike the other floors, where the doors were all closed and presumably locked, with access only being granted to holders of the proper security clearance cards, the third floor seemed to be a communal area. The doors were all open.

# LIGHTNING

"What level is the cafeteria on?" I asked.

"Third floor," Johnny said.

I leaned closer to the monitor showing the third-floor corridor. "Strange."

"What is it?" Jax asked.

"See the cafeteria door? It's open. I think it's this door here." I pointed to one of the doors leading off the deserted third-floor corridor on the other screen.

Jax nodded. "Yeah, I think that's it."

I looked at her. "So, why aren't those zombies wandering out into the corridor? We've seen how they usually act; they wander everywhere. But these are acting differently. It's like they're huddling together for protection. But there's no danger in the corridor that I can see."

Jax said, "Try some of the other rooms on that floor. There must be something there."

I pressed a button labeled *Level 3 Meeting Room 1*. The screen showed a typical meeting room with a long table running down the center of the room, chairs on either side. A large screen at the front of the room was turned off.

Pressing the next button showed us *Level 3 Meeting Room 2*. It was identical to the other meeting room, except for one thing: lying on the floor in one corner, among a mess of blood and entrails were a man and a woman. Both of them wore white lab coats, although the amount of blood made that difficult to distinguish. Their bodies lay at unnatural angles, as if they had been tossed into the corner like discarded, worn-out dolls.

"Holy fuck, they're hybrids," Sam said.

He was right; the parts of flesh that were visible in the gory mess showed the dark web of veins beneath the skin that was typical of hybrids.

Blood covered the walls in patterns that I knew from watching cop shows to be arterial sprays. A smear of it led from the bodies, across the carpet, to an area off camera.

"So now we know what the zombies are afraid of," I said. "Hybrids eat them. So all the zombies have moved into the cafeteria to stay off the dinner menu."

"Ironic," Jax said. "But what killed the hybrids?" She leaned forward and moved the joystick on the control panel, panning the camera along the bloody trail on the floor. The trail ended abruptly, and then seemed to smear up the wall. Jax panned the camera up.

The blood disappeared into a large, dark, square hole near the ceiling.

"That's the air vent, man," Sam said.

The metal grille was hanging loosely by one of its corners beneath the hole, bent out of shape as if something had smashed it open.

I sat back in my seat and looked out of the window at the building beyond the parking lot.

It seemed that patient zero had become a creature so strong and vicious that was capable of killing hybrids.

It was hunting for prey.

# LIGHTNING

And it was in the air vents.

# CHAPTER 11

E DON'T HAVE A CHOICE, man, we have to go in." Sam was pacing back and forth in front of the monitors, glancing at them every now and then. I wasn't sure if he was actually as brave as he wanted us to believe, or if he was scared and dared not show it.

"He's right," Tanya said. "It doesn't matter what's in that building, we have to go in there and get the chemical. If we don't, we're as good as dead anyway."

"Yeah, I know that," I said. "I just wish we knew where that creature was so we could avoid it."

"It won't matter," Sam said. "We'll be in and out before that…thing…even knows we're there."

"We can't just go blundering in there without knowing where it is. We'll all be killed." I wanted to add, "And then what will happen to Lucy?" but I didn't.

# LIGHTNING

"I have an idea," Jax said. "What if two people stay here and watch the cameras while the other three go inside? It might give the three people inside a better chance if they get an advance warning of what's ahead of them."

"How do we communicate?" Tanya asked.

Jax pointed at the walkie-talkies lined up in the charger.

"So who stays and who goes?" Sam asked.

"We'll draw straws," Tanya said. "There must be something we can use in here."

"There's a filing cabinet in the other room," I said. "We can cut up strips of a piece of paper."

Sam went into the other room and came back with a deck of cards. "I found these. The guards must get bored in here." He placed the deck on the table. "We all take a card. The two people who draw the highest numbers get to stay here."

It sounded reasonable enough. I cut the deck and drew a card. The three of spades. I sighed as I showed it to the others. It looked like I was going into the building.

Jax took a card, frowned, and put it face up on the table. Five of hearts.

Johnny took the nine of clubs, Tanya drew the ten of hearts, and Sam ended up with the six of diamonds.

So Tanya and Johnny were going to watch the cameras while Jax, Sam, and I went into the main building. I took a deep breath and tried to prepare myself mentally for going inside a building full of zombies, hybrids, and something that was even worse. There was nothing I could tell myself that would stop the shaking in my hands.

I put one of those hands on the Desert Eagle at my hip. If the end came while I was in that building, I was going to make sure it came quickly.

We each took a walkie-talkie and checked that they were working. Sam and Jax stuffed theirs into their backpacks and switched them off to save the batteries. I clicked mine on. We would only need one between us unless we got separated, and I had no intention of letting that happen. I clipped it to my backpack strap, on my chest, so that I didn't have to hold it. I could simply reach up and press the *Talk* button.

Tanya and Johnny took seats in front of the monitors, placing a walkie-talkie between them on the desk and turning it on. They switched two of the monitors to the *level 1 reception area*, and the *level 1 elevators*.

Sam looked at Jax and me. "Okay, guys, we can do this just like I said. A quick smash and grab. We'll be back here in ten minutes."

I wasn't sure if he was genuinely trying to psych us up, or if he was trying to reassure himself that this was going to be all right. It didn't really matter; his pep talk had zero effect on me. I was dreading going into that building, and the greatest motivational coach on earth wouldn't be able to talk me out of my fear.

LIGHTNING

I picked up my baseball bat and stepped out into the night. The drizzle had become a heavy rain, hissing down on the parking lot, pounding the cars.

"Let's move," Sam said, jogging toward the main entrance of the building.

I picked up my pace but was in no hurry to go inside, despite the rain. This might be the last time I breathed fresh air, might be the last time I was ever outdoors. Once I went through that door, I might never come back.

We reached the glass doors, and Sam swiped his card through the lock on the wall. The doors slid open with a gentle whisper. The air that drifted out between them smelled foul.

"Ready?" Sam asked. Jax nodded. I didn't feel like I would ever be ready, but I nodded, too.

We slipped into the building like thieves in the night.

# CHAPTER 12

E CROSSED THE RECEPTION AREA quickly, looking all around for any sign of movement. It was as quiet as a tomb.

The walkie-talkie crackled through the silence. "We can see you on the camera," Tanya said. "Everything looks okay."

I glanced up at the camera set high on the wall, its red light blinking. Under any other circumstances, I might have waved, but I felt too tense to do anything more than press the button on my walkie-talkie and say, "We're heading for the elevators."

We reached the three closed metal doors. Jax pushed the button and it lit up green, an upward-pointing arrow indicating the direction we would be traveling.

"Come on," Sam muttered, pacing nervously. "Where is the fucking thing? It's not like anyone else in here is using them."

We heard the elevator arrive behind the middle door, clanking noisily. The doors slid open and we stepped inside. A recorded female voice said, "Going up."

Sam hit the button for the fourth floor. The doors slid closed.

"Tanya," I said into the walkie-talkie, "we're going up to the fourth floor. Is it clear?" I had wanted to ask her that question before we were on our way—that was the idea of having them check the camera feeds, after all—but Sam had pressed the button without thinking.

"I think so," she said. "Johnny, check the level four elevators." Then she said, "Shit. No, it's not clear. There are nasties in the corridor."

I looked at the illuminated numbers over the door. The third floor came and went quickly. The next floor was the fourth. I hit the button for the fifth floor, knowing the elevator was going to stop at the fourth, but hoping it would proceed faster if it had another floor to go to.

Sam leveled the MP5 at the closed doors. "Don't worry, I've got this."

"Don't shoot if you don't have to," I said. "We don't want to make any noise that will attract that thing in the vents."

He nodded but didn't lower the weapon. "I'll only shoot if I have to."

The recorded voice said, "Fourth floor," and the doors slid apart. The corridor, which had been empty when we'd left the guard station, was teeming with zombies. Even though they were a few yards from the elevator, the stench of their rotting flesh hit me like a putrid fist.

They turned to face us, a collective moan rising from their hideous dead mouths as they sensed living prey. As I repeatedly hit the button to close the doors, I estimated there to be at least twenty nasties. Where had they come from so quickly, and why were they here?

I realized then that the stench was not only coming from the zombies; the dead, eviscerated security guards lay on the floor a few feet from the elevator door. The scene had looked bad enough in black and white on a screen; it looked a thousand times worse up close and personal.

It looked like the guards' spines had been ripped from their bodies. Their uniforms and the flesh beneath were torn open in a ragged line from the backs of their necks to their buttocks. The bodies sagged unnaturally, making me sure that the spine was gone. But with all the blood and organs everywhere, it was impossible to tell for sure.

The zombies lurched toward us.

"Get us out of here, man," Sam said.

I jabbed at the button marked "5" over and over. "The elevator's too fucking slow," I said.

Sam began shooting. In the steel elevator car, the noise was deafening. Every sound in my ears became muffled except for a sudden high-pitched ringing. Sam continued

LIGHTNING

to fire, the MP5 jerking in his hand as it shot bullet after bullet into the mass of advancing, rotting flesh. A mottled blue hand reached in through the door. I hit it with my baseball bat but the lack of space to swing the bat meant I had to jerk the bat at the hand as if I was playing cricket, slamming the fingers into the steel wall above the elevator's control panel.

Jax used her own bat to push the zombies' face out of the elevator as the doors began to slide shut.

We went up to the fifth floor.

"Tanya, what's the fifth floor like?" I asked quickly into the walkie-talkie.

"Clear," she said as the doors opened and the disembodied female voice, sounding muffled in my ringing ears, announced, "Fifth floor."

We stepped out into the corridor, weapons ready. The rooms on this level appeared to be offices. Some of the doors had metallic nameplates on them. I saw one that said, "Administration", and another that read, "Personnel".

"We need to find somewhere safe where we can discuss what to do next," I said. There was no way we were going down to the labs on the floor below until that zombie horde moved somewhere else. I wondered if they had been attracted by the smell of the dead bodies by the elevator. If so, they would feed, and then hang around the area until something stimulated them to move. That was going to be a problem.

79

Sam opened a door that was marked as belonging to a Doctor David Laurie, looked inside, and waved us over. We entered the office, which was decorated with light blue walls and a darker blue carpet. One wall was lined with a bookshelf. The books were mainly thick hardbacks with titles that looked like they related to chemistry. A light wooden desk with a computer, mouse, and keyboard sat near a window. I looked out at the view of the compound and the rolling hills beyond. The rain had smeared the glass, making the outside world seem unreal.

"What are we going to do now?" Jax asked.

Sam shrugged. "I don't know, man."

I leaned against the desk, wondering how we were going to get to the labs. "We need those zombies out of the way," I said.

"No shit, Sherlock." Sam rolled his eyes and started to read the titles of the books on the wall.

The walkie-talkie crackled. It was Johnny's voice that came over the airwaves, his smooth tone reminding me of when Lucy and I used to listen to him on Survivor Radio. I wished I was on the deck of The Big Easy now, dancing to some tune Johnny had chosen, instead of here in this facility where the virus that had destroyed the world had been created. "Alex, there's someone walking along the corridor on your level."

"Who is it?" I whispered into the walkie-talkie.

"It's that woman we saw earlier, the one with the broken glasses. She's near the elevators again."

Sam went to the door, opening it quietly. "She's there," he whispered. "She's not a zombie or anything."

I remembered the way she had been staring vacantly as she walked, her broken glasses hanging from her face. If she wasn't a nasty, then she had probably lost her mind. Still, she knew this place. She might be able to help us in some way.

"We could talk to her," I suggested to Sam.

He nodded and was about to walk out into the corridor when he suddenly stopped. His eyes widened as he saw something out there. Then he stepped back into the office and closed the door.

"What's wrong?" I asked.

His voice came out as a whisper. "Something took her, man. Something that moved so fast I barely even saw it."

Jax took the Desert Eagle from her holster and held it loosely in her right hand. Her hand was trembling, making the gun shake in her grip.

Sam backed away from the wooden door slowly, keeping the MP5 steady. "If it comes in here, I'm going to blast it," he whispered.

We stood in the office silently, waiting. I realized I was holding my breath. I wanted to contact Tanya and Johnny on the walkie-talkie but didn't dare make a sound. I was thankful that they had the good sense not to talk to us. The crackling from the walkie-talkie would alert anything in the corridor to our presence.

The rain beat on the window as if it were counting off the passing seconds.

"Do you think it's gone?" Jax whispered.

I shrugged. I could imagine it standing outside the door, waiting patiently for us to step out into the corridor. My fingers brushed lightly over the butt of the Desert Eagle at my hip. If the thing out there moved as fast as Sam said it did, I wouldn't even have time to use the gun on myself before I was torn apart like those security guards by the elevators.

I remembered that it moved through the air vents, and frantically looked for the vent in this office, breathing a sigh of relief when I saw that it was barely big enough for a rat to crawl through. The larger vents in the building were probably only in the corridors, labs, and bigger rooms like the meeting room where we had seen the dead hybrids on the monitors.

I didn't know how long we had been standing there when the walkie-talkie crackled.

It was Tanya. "It's moved away from your location. It's on level three. We just saw it run past one of the cameras there."

I breathed another sigh of relief. "We have to get that chemical and get out of here as soon as we can," I said. "Hart said that patient zero had become something more dangerous than a hybrid but he didn't say it was so fast.

"He probably didn't know," Jax said. "They would only know what the people here at Alpha Two told them. Most

LIGHTNING

people who knew how fast that creature was probably didn't live to tell the tale." She put the Desert Eagle back into her holster. "But I agree that we need to get the hell out of here as soon as we can. This place is much more dangerous than we thought."

"So what do we do, man?" Sam asked. "There's a shitload of zombies right outside the lab where the H1 is. If we go down there and start shooting, that thing might hear us and come to check out what's making all the noise. Then we're fucked."

I looked out of the window at the dark, rainy night as if it might offer some inspiration. It didn't. We couldn't just stay in this office all night; we had to make a move. Each passing second we spent in this building could too easily be our last, and my nerves were so fraught I felt like I might snap at any moment and make a mad dash for the exit.

It became all too clear why Hart had injected us with the virus; he had sent us somewhere so dangerous that any sane person would abandon the mission and run for safety. I would never do that because of Lucy, but the others would and I couldn't blame them. By injecting us with the virus, Hart was forcing us to see this mission through to the end. We had to ignore every survival instinct in our body that told us to get the hell out of Dodge. Because failing the mission would kill us anyway. We would become monsters.

*So let's get it done*, I told myself. *There has to be a way to get that chemical.*

My thoughts were interrupted when the door opened. I spun around, bringing my bat up, ready to fight. When I saw the woman who walked into the office, I lowered it.

She was in her fifties, with blonde hair that was cut short in a pixie style, and blue eyes behind thick-rimmed glasses. Her white blouse and tweed skirt made me think she was an office worker rather than a scientist, but she wore a nametag that said she was Doctor Lisa Colbert. She looked at Jax and me as she entered the room, but she didn't react to us other than to say, "This is Dave's office." It was said as a matter-of-fact statement rather than an accusation regarding our presence here.

"Doctor Colbert," I said gently, "We didn't know there were any survivors here. Is there anyone else alive in this place?"

She pondered for a moment and then shook her head. "No, only me. Nobody else made it. Vess got them all."

"What are you talking about?" Jax asked. "Who is Vess?"

Doctor Colbert turned her eyes to Jax. "Vess." She said the name in a hushed tone, as if she were afraid to speak it too loudly.

Sam raised an eyebrow. "This is bullshit. She's crazier than a box of frogs."

"Doctor Colbert, who is Vess?" I asked her, ignoring Sam.

"Vess," she whispered, turning to me, her eyes wide. Her gaze seemed to become far away, and I wondered if Sam was right and she had lost her mind. It would be understandable, being the sole survivor in a building full of monsters. She had probably known most of the people who were now roaming the corridors in various states of decay before they had become zombies. What would that do to someone's mind, to be hunted by creature that used to be friends and acquaintances?

She turned to the door and waved for us to follow her.

"I'm not following some crazy scientist," Sam said.

"Wait here, then," I told him. "She's survived for this long, maybe she knows something we don't about the building. I want to see what she's going to show us"

"Probably her collection of dismembered dolls," Sam muttered, following us out into the corridor despite his announcement that he wasn't going anywhere.

I pressed the button on the walkie-talkie. "Is level five clear?"

"Looks clear," Tanya said. "The nasties are all over those bodies on level four."

"Let me know if they move away. We need to get to that lab."

"Will do. Where's that woman taking you?"

"I'm not sure." I lowered my voice so that Doctor Colbert couldn't hear me. "She may just be crazy, or she might know something about what happened here. Probably a little of both."

"Be careful, Alex."

"Of course."

Doctor Colbert led us to an office door bearing the name Doctor Marcus Vess. She opened the door and stepped inside, gesturing for us to follow.

The office was identical to Doctor Laurie's office, even down to the books on the shelf, which I was sure from the unpronounceable titles were the same ones as on Laurie's shelves.

Doctor Colbert took a seat behind the desk and typed something on the keyboard. Turning the screen so we could all see it, she pointed at a picture of a dark-haired man in his thirties, dressed in a shirt and tie beneath a white lab coat, looking at the camera. He seemed to be in this office at the time. The image was actually a video. "This is Doctor Marcus Vess," Colbert said. She pressed the play icon and Vess began to speak to the camera.

"This is a historic day," he said. "The lab trials of the serum have been inconclusive on mice and rats, but I know that's only because I developed it to combat CJD in human beings. Animal testing will never show us what can be achieved. The only way to do that is to perform a human trial. I spoke to Akers about it, but she has requested more testing in the lab before we even think about injecting the serum into a human being, even someone who has Creutzfeldt-Jakob disease and is willing to take part in a trial. She says we can't go ahead until we're sure how the serum behaves in the human body."

He paused to look out of his window. Sunlight streamed into the office, brightening the pale blue wall behind him. "How can we be sure until we administer it to a patient? If I don't get results soon, I'll lose my funding for this project and they'll put me to work on something else. I'm making a breakthrough here, but Akers can't see it because she's too busy attending board meetings and making decisions that she has no right to make."

Leaning in closer to the camera, he lowered his voice. "I'm going to inject myself with the serum today. Akers needs to be shown that it's perfectly harmless in humans. Once she realizes that, we can move the project forward. It's been delayed enough as it is." He reached forward, and the video ended.

Doctor Colbert used the mouse to bring up another video. This one was recorded in a bedroom. Vess was sitting at the edge of the bed, dressed only in boxers, looking like he had a bad case of the flu. His eyes were bloodshot, his face drawn and tired. When he spoke, he sounded like his sinuses were blocked. "I made a mistake. I didn't realize I was coming down with the flu when I injected the serum. It's been going around the facility, so I should have been more wary of the possibility that I'd caught it. If it wasn't for Akers and her deadlines, I'd have waited." He looked angrily at the camera.

"I think the serum is reacting with the flu virus. The vascularity in my arms is very pronounced." He raised his arm to show the camera that the veins beneath the skin in his arm were dark and prominent.

"This has nothing to do with the serum," he said. "I'm having a bad reaction to it because of the flu, not because the serum itself is harmful in any way. Akers won't believe that, of course. She'll try to stop my funding. Well, she can fuck off. Everybody can just fuck off." He got off the bed and stormed across the room, beyond the view of the camera. I heard something smash. Vess appeared again a moment later with bloody grazes on his fist. "It's just the flu," he said before switching off the camera.

"Wow," Sam said. "It looks like this dude fucked up big time."

Colbert looked at each of us. "Do you want to see the rest?"

"We know how this one ends," Sam said.

"We still want to see some more," I told her. I had been led to believe that the zombie virus had been developed in a government lab, but now it looked like a harmless serum had reacted with the flu virus in the outside world. There wasn't some diabolical government plot to create monsters; the whole thing had just been a huge mistake.

Doctor Colbert brought up another video and pressed play. This one was filmed in the bedroom again. Vess looked bleary-eyed as he looked into the camera. Only his face and the collar of his shirt were visible. "I went out tonight. I don't know why. I still feel ill, and I've not

LIGHTNING

returned to work yet. But I remember thinking I needed to get some fresh air, and see other people." He paused and looked down for a moment before facing the camera again. "That's the last thing I remember. I must have blacked out. I don't know where I went, or how I got back home. But something has happened." He moved the camera back, revealing that his shirt was covered with blood. "I don't think it's mine," he said. "I can't remember what I've done." The video ended.

"There's one more," Colbert said. "Vess came back here, saying he needed to be treated in our hospital. After he explained that he had injected himself with the serum he had developed for the treatment of CJD, he was taken to the hospital wing to be monitored.

"What we saw alarmed us. Vess was showing signs of paranoia, loss of cognitive function, and violent tendencies. He had been away from here for a week, mingling with the general population. If the virus in his system was contagious, we had no hope for containment. We had no idea where he had been during that week, and Vess was in no condition to tell us.

"The virus in his body was previously unknown, so we took a video record of his deterioration." She pressed play on another video. Vess was in a hospital bed, surrounded by doctors, nurses, and scientists. His eyes were yellow, his skin pale. The veins in his neck and face were clearly visible. He was writhing in the bed as if in pain, sweat covering his face.

A voice off-camera said, "Video record of patient Doctor Marcus Vess. The patient is exhibiting signs of rage and paranoia. Treatment will involve…" The voice stopped as Vess grabbed the arm of a nurse and bit into her flesh. She screamed, trying to pull away. Everyone in the room moved forward to restrain Vess, but he released the nurse and turned his attention to one of the doctors, grabbing the man's lapels to pull him down and clamp his mouth around his neck.

The man behind the camera must have rushed in to help, knocking the camera to the floor as he moved past it. The picture fell from the scene on bed and showed only the tiled floor while screams and shouts could be heard in the room.

Doctor Colbert turned off the video. "I'm sure you can guess the rest. The virus began to spread around the building. We tried to contain it, but every time we thought we had it under control, we were wrong. At the same time, we began receiving reports of infected persons in the general population outside the building, in the local community. A team was dispatched to Vess's house. Some of his neighbors were missing. He had done a good job of spreading the virus before coming back to us."

"So he was patient zero," I said.

She nodded. "Yes, he is."

"Is?" Sam asked. "Don't tell me that fucker is still alive."

# LIGHTNING

She looked at him and nodded. "He's still alive," she said. "I think he's in the air vents."

# CHAPTER 13

HE WALKIE-TALKIE CRACKLED. TANYA said, "Alex, we have a problem."

I pressed the button. "What is it?"

"About two dozen zombies have just wandered onto your floor from the stairs. They're hanging around by the elevators. Some of them are coming down the corridor outside the offices."

"We're going to get trapped in here," I told the others. "They could be wandering around out there for days. That's time we don't have."

"Let's go kick some ass," Sam said.

I contacted Tanya again. "We need a clear escape route off this floor."

"Hold on, we'll check the cameras." The walkie-talkie went quiet for a minute. I could hear shuffling sounds beyond the door.

LIGHTNING

I turned the walkie-talkie's volume down. No need to advertise our presence in here.

"It doesn't look good," Tanya said. "There are nasties by the elevator and on the stairs. I can't see a way off that floor that doesn't involve running into a lot of zombies."

Johnny's voice cut in. "Wait a minute. Alex, there's another set of stairs on the other side of the building. I think it's an emergency exit." I heard papers being moved as he checked the maps. "Yeah, it runs all the way down to the first floor."

"Are there any cameras in there?" I asked. "I'd like to know what's there before we go running into it."

"No cameras," Johnny said.

While the conversation was going on, Jax had opened up her map and laid it on Vess's desk. She ran her finger along the corridors and rooms until she found the emergency stairs that Johnny was talking about. "We need to get past the elevators and into this corridor here," she said, tracing her finger along the route we were going to have to take.

"We're going to have to fight our way through," I said. "We don't have a choice." I looked at Doctor Colbert. "You're going to need a weapon."

She shook her head. "I'm not going anywhere."

"You can't stay here. There are zombies right outside that door."

As if to prove my point, a thud sounded against the wood. They had heard us.

93

"It was always just a matter of time," Colbert said. "Everyone else has been killed. I was just waiting for my turn."

"You don't need to do that," I said. "We can escape."

Another thud shook the door.

"Escape to where?" she asked. "I know what's happened to the world beyond these walls. It's no better than in here. Everyone I've ever known is dead. Even if we get past those monsters outside the door, there's a much worse monster hunting us down. Vess will catch us sooner or later."

"I'm not leaving you here," I said, grabbing her arm and pulling her to her feet. I couldn't open that door knowing that the zombies would come into the office and find Doctor Colbert. Every fiber of my being told me that I had to deny those creatures the life of a human being, even if that person wanted to die. The zombie apocalypse was a war of attrition; for every human we lost, they gained another monster. I wouldn't let Lisa Colbert become one of them.

I grabbed her shoulders and looked into her eyes. "If you won't fight, then at least run."

She nodded, seemingly surprised by my determination to keep her alive.

"Are we ready, man?" Sam asked. He held the MP5 steady, muzzle pointed at the closed door.

The zombies began to pound on the door with their fists.

## LIGHTNING

"How much ammo do you have left?" I asked Sam.

"It's getting low. But we need to shoot our way out of here."

I nodded.

Jax opened the door. The zombies in the corridor fought to come inside, to taste our flesh.

The sound of the MP5 was loud in the small office but not as deafening as it had been in the elevator. As Sam delivered headshot after headshot, the nasties dropped to the floor and lay there in rotting heaps of mottled blue flesh.

Sam ran forward, stepped over the carcasses, and began firing down the corridor toward the elevators. We followed, Doctor Colbert allowing me to drag her along by the hand.

At the far end of the corridor, a horde of nasties began shambling in our direction. Sam shot three of them, and they fell quickly as their brains were destroyed, but then the MP5 made an empty clicking noise. "Fuck!" Sam shouted.

"We need to turn right by the elevators," Jax said as we moved forward.

I had to let go of Colbert's hand as we got near the nasties so that I could use both hands to wield the bat. To my relief, she stayed close behind me. I had been afraid that she might just stand where she was, refusing to move, but she seemed to have decided to live a little longer.

I swung the bat at the head of the closest zombie, a man in a white lab coat whose face was hanging off his skull loosely, chewed and torn. His head caved in with a sickening crack as the bat smashed through bone and brain.

Jax and Sam were likewise swinging their bats, clearing a path past the nasties.

A blonde woman in a black blouse and skirt lunged at me, teeth bared. I pushed her back with the tip of the bat before swinging it into her head as hard as I could. Her skull cracked open, spilling liquid and brains as she fell to the floor.

"Oh, my God, that was Linda," Colbert said, her hand flying to her mouth and her eyes wide.

We fought our way around the corner and into the corridor that led away from the elevators to the part of the building where we would find the emergency stairs.

The corridor was clear. We ran.

The zombies followed at their deathly pace, a collective moan rising from them as if they were pleading with us to come back and let them eat us.

We reached a closed, locked, metal and glass door. Jax used her access card to open it and we slipped through. The door closed behind us. The zombies pressed themselves against the glass in vain, watching us with their hateful yellow eyes as we walked away.

I noticed a camera on the wall at the end of the corridor. "Can you see where we are?" I asked into the walkie-talkie.

Johnny answered. "Yeah, it looks clear. The door to the stairs should be on your left."

We found it. The door was a regular door with a sign that showed a stickman going down a flight of stairs beneath the words EMERGENCY EXIT.

"What's the fourth floor like now?" I asked Johnny.

"Still a whole lot of nastiness going on at the elevators."

"What's in the corridor directly below us? If we take these stairs down to the fourth floor, where will we come out?"

"Let me just check that." There was a pause while he checked the map. "Looks like labs. Most of the fourth floor consists of labs."

"Can you check the area where the emergency stairs come out on that level? Assuming the stairs and elevators are in the same relative positions as they are on this floor, we should be far enough away from the elevators to avoid attracting the attention of the nasties there."

Johnny said, "Tanya, can you find a camera for this corridor here?" I assumed he was showing her the map. A few seconds later, he said to me, "The corridor looks okay."

"Is there a locked access door between the elevators and the emergency stairs on that floor, the same as there is on this one?" I looked along the corridor at the zombies still trying to reach us by pressing themselves against the metal and glass door.

"Yeah, looks like it."

"I have an idea," I said to Jax, Sam, and Colbert.

I opened the door to the emergency stairs. The stairs were made of steel and led down to the fourth floor as well as up to the roof. We descended them slowly, wary of any movement below us. But the stairs seemed deserted. When we opened the fourth floor door, it revealed a corridor identical to the one we had just left. Except the doors here were all digitally locked and led to labs. Through the glass panels in the doors, I could see white-tiled rooms containing various machines, steel worktables, and glass cabinets full of chemicals.

Through the access door halfway along the corridor, I could see the pack of zombies at the elevators, still feeding from the dead bodies of the security guards.

I removed my backpack and found the waterproof matches I had brought from Apocalypse Island. "This should make them move," I said. "And they can't come this way because of that door." I struck a match and reached up toward the ceiling where a sprinkler sensor was located.

An alarm sounded and a red light above the emergency exit door came on. The sprinklers went into action, raining water down on us from the ceiling.

When the water hit the zombies, they left their feast and shuffled through a set of swinging doors that led to the main stairs.

"I don't understand," Doctor Colbert said, watching them through the glass door. "What's happening?"

"They hate water," I replied, putting the matches into the pocket of my jeans. "I think it's something to do with the virus trying to keep the host body from rotting quicker. When it rains, the zombies seek shelter."

"So they have a weakness," she whispered, almost to herself.

When the area was clear, we opened the access door and walked along the corridor, through the spray of water, to the elevators. The bodies of the security guards had almost been picked clean, their bones clearly visible. I had been right; the spines had been ripped out and were missing. The chill that ran through my body had nothing to do with the coldness of the water that was raining down on us.

We found the lab that Hart had told us contained the H1NZ1 at the end of the corridor. Sam opened the door with his access card and we went inside.

The lab was large, clinically clean, and smelled strongly of bleach. The white tiles and stainless steel surfaces shone beneath the overhead lights. The sprinklers weren't on in here; the system was smart enough to know that the "fire" was in the fourth floor corridor. The alarm was still ringing outside, but with the door closed, it sounded far away.

I turned to Doctor Colbert. "Do you know where the H1NZ1 is kept?"

She nodded. "In the supply room there." She pointed to a doorway that led into a smaller room of shelves stacked with plastic containers and cardboard boxes. "I don't understand. What are you doing here, and what do you want with the H1NZ1?"

"We're from Site Alpha One," I said as we went to the supply room. "We've come to collect the H1NZ1 because the scientists there need it."

"Site Alpha One is still in operation?" she asked. "Being on an island they would have more chance of survival, but there was a cross-contamination of both sites because staff moved between them as required. When we lost contact with them, we thought the site had been overrun."

"They had problems," I said, "but the building is secure."

"And the labs are still running?" she asked.

"Yes. That's why they want the H1NZ1; the scientists at Alpha One have worked out a way to make an antivirus from it."

We entered the room and Colbert went to a shelf that held hundreds of small metallic boxes. "It's in here," she said. "Each box holds a single vial." As we began loading them into our backpacks, she said, "That means they've been working on the problem all this time. At Site Alpha One, I mean. We thought that after the vaccine failed to

LIGHTNING

work properly, and the zombies and hybrids took over this building, that was the end of everything. I had no idea they had developed an antivirus."

"Yeah, apparently they have," I said, stuffing handfuls of the metallic boxes into my pack. They were light enough that I could hardly tell they had anything inside. "But we need to get this stuff to them so they can produce it."

Tears appeared in her eyes. "I thought everything had been destroyed. I thought that all of our work had ended. I was waiting to die and all this time, Alpha One was still operational and working on a solution. Do you people work for the security firm?"

Sam grunted and then said, "No, we don't work for those fuckers at all."

Colbert looked confused. "I don't understand. You're doing this for them but you don't work for them?"

"We were coerced into coming here," Jax said. She had filled her pack and slung it over her shoulder. "If we don't get these chemicals back to Alpha One, we're all going to become hybrids."

Colbert looked shocked. "They let you get bitten?"

Sam rolled his eyes. "Worse than that, man. They injected us with the fucking virus."

"Oh, my God," she said with a tremor in her voice. "You're not ill so you must have been injected with the pure strain. What color was it? It's very important that you remember."

"It was pale blue," I said.

"When were you injected?"

"A few hours ago," I said.

She nodded. "We must get these vials to Site Alpha One immediately."

"They're sending a chopper to pick us up the day after tomorrow," Jax said.

Colbert shook her head. "No, that's much too late. We need to go now."

"We can't," I said. "They won't be back here until 1300 hours on Tuesday. We can't change that."

"No, you don't understand," she protested. "You've been injected with the pure strain. You don't have that much time."

"Look, lady," Sam said, "We know it takes four days to turn into a hybrid. They gave us the pure blue shit so that we won't get sick in the meantime. It's all under control."

She marched out of the supply room and into the lab, leaning on the edge of a steel table as if to steady herself. "Listen to me very closely. Please. The people at Alpha One don't know what an injection of the pure strain does. We hypothesized that a vaccinated person who received a dose of the pure version of the virus would turn into a Type 3 in four days. It was all theory."

"Type 3?" Jax asked.

"Yes, Type 3." Colbert went to a whiteboard on the wall, picked up a marker and wrote "Type 1" near the top. Below that, she wrote "Type 2", and below that "Type 3".

"What you call a hybrid is a Type 3," she said, pointing at the bottom of the board. She wrote the word "vaccine" next to Type 3.

Pointing to the middle of the board, where she had written Type 2, she said, "The Type 2 is the undead zombie." She wrote the words "No vaccine" and "bite".

"When we were still in contact with Site Alpha One, we had a joint project to produce a pure strain of the virus. This is not the serum that Vess injected into himself; it's the result of that serum combining with the H1N1 flu virus that was already present in his body. We wanted to be able to produce the pure virus so that we could study it and look for a way to kill it.

"At the time, the question came up of how this pure strain would react with the faulty vaccine that causes hybrids. We decided that it would have the same effect as the virus that is transmitted by a bite and the victim would become a hybrid. But because of the absence of some impurities that are transmitted from the biter to the victim, we decided that the transformation into a Type 3 wouldn't involve the usual four-day sickness."

"So there's nothing to worry about," Sam said.

"We were wrong," Doctor Colbert said. "After the two sites lost contact with each other, we did some further studies here at Alpha Two. We went beyond simple theory and performed a series of experiments in this lab to find out what would happen if a vaccinated person were injected with the pure strain of the virus.

"The experiments had no real-world application; we didn't think anyone would actually ever be injected with the virus—why would they? But scientific curiosity drove us to seek answers anyway. The results were conclusive; the vaccine has no effect whatsoever on the pure virus."

Next to "Type 1" on the board, she wrote the word "Pure".

"So that is how we classify the infected. When the virus is transmitted by a bite or scratch to an unvaccinated person, that person dies, and a Type 2 is created. A zombie. Add the vaccine into the mix, and that creates a victim who remains alive, but becomes driven by a homicidal rage. That is a Type 3. A hybrid."

She pointed at the top of the board. "But if someone is injected with the pure virus, they become a Type 1. At the moment, there is only one Type 1 in existence...Vess."

"So if we don't get the antivirus that this H1NZ1 is needed for, we'll become like him?" Jax asked.

Doctor Colbert nodded.

"Okay," I said, "But we're going to be given the antivirus when we get back to Alpha One, so why panic?"

"Tell me exactly when you were injected with the pure virus. What time was it?" Colbert asked.

I shrugged. "I didn't check my watch."

"It was eight thirty," Jax said. "There was a clock in the room, and I noticed it said eight thirty."

On the whiteboard, Colbert wrote "Introduction of virus: 2030 hrs Sunday." She drew a vertical line beneath

LIGHTNING

the words and asked, "What time is your rendezvous with the people from Alpha One?"

I told her, and she wrote "1300 hrs. Tuesday" at the bottom of the vertical line.

She said, "That would be plenty of time if you had been bitten, or if our original theories about the pure virus were correct. You'd be able to return to Alpha One and receive the antivirus with time to spare. From the time you were injected, you would have ninety-six hours before becoming a Type 3."

"You're saying we don't have that long," I said.

Shaking her head, she drew a horizontal line halfway up the vertical line and wrote "2230 hrs. Monday" next to it.

"The people who injected you were working on outdated information regarding the pure strain of the virus. This is when you'll turn," she said. "Tomorrow night at ten thirty. You don't have anywhere near the ninety-six hours that the people at Alpha One thought you'd have. The pure virus works much faster than that."

She checked the clock on the wall. "You have twenty-four hours left."

# CHAPTER 14

I DON'T FUCKING BELIEVE THIS," Sam said, throwing his backpack to the floor. "I knew we'd get screwed over by those fuckers on Apocalypse Island." He paced back and forth along the length of the lab, muttering to himself.

"They didn't know anything about it," I reminded him. "They thought that everything they told us about the virus was correct."

"Just shut the fuck up, Alex."

I decided to let him work out his anger issues by himself. I didn't want another punch to the gut.

Jax was standing by the window, looking out at the rainy night. I went over to her. "Hey, are you okay?"

She nodded but didn't say anything.

"We'll get through this," I said. I didn't really believe those words, not at that moment. We were only twenty-four hours from becoming creatures like the thing in the vents.

Jax sighed. "I don't think so. Not this time, Alex. I'm going to die not knowing if my boyfriend is still alive or not. I'll never know what happened to him. And he'll never know what happened to me."

"Don't think like that," I said. "This isn't over yet." I was trying to reassure Jax but I was in exactly the same situation; if I didn't get that antivirus, and turned in twenty-four hours, I would never know what had become of Joe and my parents. Lucy's fate, on the other hand, was certain; she would turn. I guessed that the guards at Alpha One would kill her once she ceased being a human being. Hart's wife, Kate, would suffer the same fate.

An idea came into my head. It was probably too late for me, but if I could get my backpack full of H1NZ1 to the rendezvous site, Hart would find it and take it back to Apocalypse Island. Lucy and Kate could be saved, even if we couldn't.

Jax reached inside her T-shirt and pulled on the thin gold chain she wore around her neck. "Derek gave me this," she said "He asked me to marry him." A diamond engagement ring hung from the chain, sparkling in the lab's artificial light. "I never wore it because I couldn't decide if I was going to say yes. I was an idiot. I should have said yes without even a second thought. I didn't realize how precious our time together was. I didn't know it was going to end so suddenly." Her shoulders began to hitch. I put my arms around her and let her cry against my chest.

I liked Jax. At times, she seemed to be the most vulnerable person in the group, and that was endearing. Even though she could be damn tough sometimes, she wasn't in the same league as Tanya. Jax showed her softer side sometimes, and the fact that she wasn't afraid to show it made me like her even more.

It felt good to hold another person, even if it was someone I really didn't know. In the midst of death, destruction, and a countdown to our own demise, there was comfort in the touch of another human being.

The moment was ruined when Sam kicked a steel worktable with the toe of his boot. The sound reverberated through the lab.

Jax pulled back from me with a little smile, and turned to face Sam. "What's wrong with you?"

"This is some fucked-up shit, man. I don't want to die here."

Doctor Colbert spoke up. "I thought you people were fighters. I'd never seen a more motivated group of survivors. I was barely surviving here, thinking I was going to die, but you convinced me to try to live again. You showed me that the zombies have a weakness, and told me that there are still scientists at Alpha One working on a solution to the problem we face. You gave me hope. Now you're giving up? You have twenty-four hours left; are you going to spend them doing nothing but waiting to die?"

"She's right," Jax said, wiping tears from her face. "I don't want to sit here doing nothing while time ticks away. There must be something we can do, something we can try."

I asked Colbert, "Is there any way we can communicate with Alpha One from this facility?"

"No, we tried that. When they didn't answer our calls, we assumed the island had been taken over by the zombies. We had problems of our own, so contacting Alpha One wasn't exactly a priority."

"And there's no other way to speak with them?"

She shook her head. "No. We kept in contact via telephone, email, and video calls, but it all stopped suddenly. Our network went down."

So, communication with Alpha One seemed to be out of the question.

"How far is it to the coast?" I asked.

"About seventy miles."

"We can get there by car," I said.

"This is bullshit," Sam said. "When we get to the coast, then what? Do you think we're just going to find a boat to take us to Apocalypse Island?"

"I'll row there in a dingy if it means saving our lives," I replied.

"Don't be stupid, man. We'd get to the coast and we'd be stuck there. And don't forget that there are soldiers crawling all over the coast. We'd get captured before we even reached the beach."

109

"We'll have to come up with a plan," I said, "but first let's get out of this building and back to the guard station. Tanya and Johnny deserve to know the situation, and maybe they'll have some ideas on what we can do about it."

Sam continued pacing back and forth. "We're all fucked."

"When did you become such a pessimist?" I asked him. I wasn't sure what had happened to Sam lately, but he had changed from the easy-going, levelheaded man I had once known. He had always been impetuous and brave, but there had been an underlying calm in his nature. And as a cameraman for survivalist Vigo Johnson, he had surely been in some harrowing situations, yet he seemed not to be affected by them or anything we had encountered together. But since being injected with the virus, the calmness had been replaced with anger. Maybe he had only fooled us into believing he'd had his shit together, and the facade was now slipping.

"When did you become such an optimist?" he threw back at me. "When we met you, you were whining about everything. Now you're all 'fuck yeah, let's do it.' You've changed, man."

I wasn't sure he meant it as a compliment, but I took it as one. I remembered complaining about everything all the time. I wasn't sure what had changed inside me, but now I hardly saw any point in griping about the little things that annoyed me. The things I used to complain about paled in

LIGHTNING

comparison to the big problems I had to deal with now. Maybe, like Jax, I had realized that life was precious.

I didn't want to waste any of that precious time, even if I only had twenty-four hours of it left. Especially if I only had twenty-four hours of it left.

Maybe I could at least get the H1NZ1 to the helipad where Hart would be landing in a couple of days' time. Doctor Colbert could tell him what had happened, and fly to Apocalypse Island with the chemical to do some good. Maybe she would be a part of the team that would finally figure out how to deal with the zombies for good.

Jax leaned against the lab table as if she had suddenly lost all her strength. I put a hand on her shoulder. "Are you okay?"

She clutched her right arm, pain etched across her ashen face as she shook her head. "No," she said through gritted teeth. She doubled over, falling to the floor, moaning in agony.

"What's wrong with her?" I asked Doctor Colbert desperately.

She shrugged. "I don't know. Maybe she's reacting badly to the virus."

"I'm okay," Jax said. "Help me up."

She took my hand and I helped her get to her feet. She leaned on the table, breathing deeply. Beads of sweat had broken out across her forehead.

I put an arm around her, but she shook it off. "I'm fine," she said.

I didn't know what was happening to her, but I decided that we should get out of here as soon as possible and regroup with Tanya and Johnny in the security-guard station.

I went to the door and looked out at the corridor. It seemed deserted. I pressed the button on the walkie-talkie.

"How does the fourth floor look from the cameras?" If this floor was clear, all we had to do was ride the elevator down to the reception area and get the hell out of the building.

There was no answer other than static.

I tried again. "Tanya? Johnny?"

Nothing.

Then Tanya's voice came over the airwaves, sounding worried. "Alex, there's something…we don't know what it is…but it just ran past one of the cameras on your floor."

"What? Where?" I looked out at the corridor again. "I can't see anything."

"It was by the elevators," Tanya said. "I'm panning the camera around but I can't see it anywhere. It moved too fast."

I turned to the others. "What do you think? Should we wait, or go now?"

"Let's go," Sam said, "I'm sick of this place. There's too much science everywhere." He looked at Colbert. "No offense, lady."

Jax nodded. "I want to get out of here, too."

LIGHTNING

Doctor Colbert said, "I'll go along with whatever you decide."

"Okay, let's do it." I opened the lab door and we went out into the corridor. The sprinklers had stopped, but the walls were dripping with water, and there was at least an inch of it covering the floor. I went ahead, moving as quickly as I could while still being alert and wary. I wanted to get out of here as much as everyone else, but I didn't want to go rushing into trouble.

We got halfway along the corridor, the elevators in sight ahead, when a crashing sound made me turn around. The grille of the air vent in the corridor had hit the wall and fallen to the floor. A shape leaped out of the hole and landed in the corridor.

It was obviously Doctor Marcus Vess. His face was lined with dark veins, his eyes yellow, but I recognized him from the videos. He was naked, his entire body's vascularity prominent and dark beneath his skin. He was covered with blood, some of it dried, some fresh. He grinned at us.

"Run!" I shouted. I turned and splashed toward the elevators as fast as I could.

When I reached the elevators, I took a left turn toward the main stairs. If I had turned right, I would have hit the locked access door, and I wasn't sure if I would have time to swipe my card through the lock before Vess caught up with us.

113

But when I barged through the swing doors, I realized my mistake; the stairs were swarming with zombies, probably the ones that had been driven here by the sprinklers. I tried to halt my forward momentum but barreled into an undead woman dressed in a lab coat. She snarled at me and tried to bite my face. I pushed her away with my bat, wincing at the fetid smell that seeped from her decaying flesh.

Sam came through the door and started swinging his bat. I heard the dense wood make contact with rotten flesh as zombies began falling onto the stairs.

There were too many zombies for us to fight our way through, and Vess must be right behind us. I backed out through the doors into the corridor and turned to face Vess. He wasn't there. He was running toward the access door, where Jax was desperately sliding her card through the lock, her blue eyes wide as she watched Vess get closer.

For some reason, she had turned right where we had turned left.

The doors mercifully opened. Jax ran through. The doors closed before Vess reached them.

Through the glass, I could see Jax look over her shoulder, slowing her pace as she realized Vess hadn't made it through the door. She made it to the end of the corridor before she winced, grabbing her right arm and doubling over just as she had in the lab. She leaned against the wall, grimacing.

LIGHTNING

I was sure Vess was going to come back this way. We had no chance to get to Jax, but the emergency stairs door was on her side of the access door. If Johnny or Tanya could come up those stairs, they could get Jax to safety.

I hit the button on the walkie-talkie. "Jax is in trouble."

"Johnny is already on his way," Tanya replied. "As soon as he saw her heading for that door, he was out of here and running into the building."

The doors behind us swung open and the zombies came shuffling through, moaning and reaching for us. We backed away toward the elevators. I shot a glance over my shoulder, preparing myself for when Vess finally turned around and came for us.

But he didn't do that. After watching Jax for a moment, he climbed up into an air vent.

"Oh, fuck," I said, "he's going to come out on the other side of the door."

Jax was still leaning against the wall in obvious pain. She slid down the wall, clutching her stomach. She was helpless.

An air vent on the other side of the access door smashed open and Vess jumped down into the corridor, his feet splashing the water on the floor.

Seeing that he was on the same side of the door as her, Jax tried to crawl away.

Vess walked forward toward her as if he had all the time in the world.

115

The emergency stairs door burst open between them and Johnny appeared, Desert Eagle in his hands. He pointed it at Vess and shot.

Vess went down, falling backward into the water and lying still.

As the zombies advanced, we backed up past the elevators and into the corridor Jax had taken when I had stupidly headed for the zombie-infested main stairs.

"We might as well go this way," I told Sam and Doctor Colbert. "The zombies are blocking the elevators now." The threat from Vess seemed to be over. Now all we had to do was get to those emergency stairs and out of the building. We could figure out later how to get to Apocalypse Island.

We turned and started heading for the access door. Through the glass in the door, I could see Johnny carefully approaching Vess's unmoving body, the Desert Eagle shaking a little in his hands. Beyond him, Jax was sitting in the water on the floor, her face ghostly white. Her eyes were shut tight, her features twisted with pain. If her pain was brought on by the virus in her system, I wasn't sure she had even the twenty-four hours Doctor Colbert had promised us.

As Johnny got close to Vess, he bent over to look at the creature's face.

Vess shot his arm up and grabbed Johnny around the throat, lifting him into the air. He got to his feet, still holding Johnny up above his head. I ran for the access door, pulling my Desert Eagle from its holster. My other hand dug the door card out of my pocket.

Despite her pain, Jax had managed to get her gun into her hands. She lifted it and aimed at Vess, who moved a struggling Johnny into her line of fire. Jax hesitated.

Vess thrust his hand into the back of Johnny's neck before pulling down viciously. Johnny's eyes went wide, his mouth falling open as Vess tore his spine from his body. Tossing Johnny's dead body aside, Vess advanced on Jax.

Obviously realizing that shooting at Vess was pointless after he had dodged Johnny's bullet at close range, Jax scrambled to her feet and ran, almost slipping over on the wet floor as she turned a corner at the end of the corridor. Vess followed.

"No!" I shouted as I reached the door. My hand was shaking so much that my first attempt to swipe my card through the lock failed. I tried again, looking at Johnny's lifeless body through the glass. The water around him was stained red. The look of shock and agony on his face remained even in death.

The door opened.

I ran through, past Johnny to the end of the corridor. Jax had turned right, so I did the same, expecting to come upon her body around the corner. She wasn't fast enough to outrun Vess. Unless she had found a locked room to hole up in, she must be dead.

She was there, but she was alive. Kneeling in the water, tears streaming from her face, she held the gun in her hand up in the air in front of her, but her hand was shaking so badly that the muzzle of the Desert Eagle swung wildly left and right.

Vess was gone, his exit route marked by a broken air vent in the wall.

Why had he left Jax alive?

I went to her, putting my arm around her and helping her to stand. Her entire body was trembling like a leaf held to a branch by such a fragile connection that the slightest breeze would blow it away.

She leaned against me as if she had lost the strength to stand.

"We need to get out of here," I told Sam.

He nodded, eyeing the broken air vent warily. We took Jax between us, moving back along the corridor as fast as we could. Doctor Colbert led the way, her own body trembling almost as much as Jax's. I imagined that she must have seen some grisly sights since the outbreak, but seeing a living man's spine being ripped out wasn't one of them. I tried not to think about it but the image of Johnny's face kept flashing into my mind.

We reached the emergency stairs and began to descend. Jax found her strength by the time we reached the second floor. She murmured, "I'm okay," and supported herself on the metal railing as we went down to the first floor.

# LIGHTNING

The door opened onto a first-floor corridor that led to an access door. We went through it and into the reception area, which was still deserted.

As we went through the main doors and out into the rainy night, I breathed the cool, fresh air thankfully. I had wondered, before entering the building, if I would ever leave. I had made it out alive, but we had lost Johnny Drake.

His voice had lifted my spirits so many times in the past, and now I would never hear it again.

# CHAPTER 15

HE RAIN WAS STILL COMING down in force, blown into our faces by a cold wind that whistled along the edge of the building. The stars and moon were blotted out by storm clouds. As we crossed the parking lot, a flash of lightning illuminated the distant hills. A couple of seconds later, thunder rolled over the compound.

Tanya opened the door to the guard station as we approached. The pool of light coming from within the little building looked warm and welcoming. After we had piled into the room, I sat by the radiator, shivering wetly in its heat.

Jax dropped into one of the chairs, leaning heavily against the desk. She looked better than she had earlier, but I could see she was still fighting against some sort of pain.

# LIGHTNING

"I should have come to help you," Tanya said to Jax, "But Johnny was determined. He ran across to the building as soon as he knew you were in trouble. His last act was a heroic one."

Jax nodded. "He tried to save my life but lost his instead. I'll never forget that." Her voice was low, her eyes locked on the floor at her feet. I wondered if she was in shock.

Hell, after what we had just been through, we were all in shock.

An air of solemnity descended over the room. Even Sam was quiet.

I hadn't known Johnny for long, but his voice on the radio had lifted my spirits many times. Some of my best memories were of dancing to some tune or other that Johnny was playing. His rich voice, floating over the airwaves like silk, had been calm and comforting at a time when everyday living was full of stress. With the passing of Johnny Drake, we had lost a man who had done more good for the survivors of the apocalypse than anyone, simply by being there when we needed to hear a familiar voice or lose ourselves to music.

I closed my eyes and leaned against the radiator, letting the heat seep into my damp clothes and hair.

While Jax and Doctor Colbert brought Tanya up to date with exactly what had happened inside the building, I checked the time on my watch and put it into countdown mode, beginning at twenty-three hours. I wasn't sure why I did it except that I wanted to know when my final seconds were approaching.

Sam came over and sat next to me. "Hey, Alex, don't hog all the heat, man."

I gave him a flat smile but said nothing. We'd had some disagreements since coming here, and I felt uneasy when he was around me. I didn't want to say the wrong thing and be on the receiving end of another gut punch.

As if reading my mind, he said, "How's your stomach?"

"I'll live," I said. The truth was, my stomach muscles were still sore where he had hit me.

"I'm sorry about that," Sam said.

I raised an eyebrow. "You're sorry that I'll live?"

He grinned, and I saw the old Sam return. "Nah, I'm sorry I hit you, man."

"Don't worry about it." Then I decided to risk another punch and said, "We're all pissed off with this virus situation but you seemed more pissed off than anyone. What's got you so mad?"

"I can't stand having my freedom taken away from me, man. Before the shit hit the fan, when I was working as a cameraman with Vigo in the jungle, or in the desert, I felt so free. Like I didn't have to answer to anyone, you know? My old man used to work for a big corporation, and his whole life revolved around his job. He was the original corporate yes man, and the company came before anything, even his wife and his sons."

"Sons," I said. "You have a brother?"

He nodded. "I have two. One of them, my older brother, is in the army, stationed in the Middle East, so he's probably safe." He laughed. "That shows how bad things are here when being in a warzone in the Middle East is safer than being in Britain. My younger brother is a corporate man just like dear old dad. He works in New York and he probably treats his family just as badly as our dad treated us.

"I hate all that bullshit, man. I've never gone down the route of a nine to five job. And I couldn't join the army like my older brother either; I'm not good at taking orders. So I've been working freelance all my life. I probably made less money that way but at least I was my own boss and I didn't have to clock in. Being forced to work for the authorities doesn't sit well with me, man."

"This will soon be over one way or another," I reminded him.

"Yeah, we know how this is going to end, Alex. If we had stayed away from that island, we'd be on the waves right now, as free as birds."

"We would," I said, "but Lucy wouldn't."

"No, she wouldn't." He looked down at the floor and sadness passed over his face. "It's good that you're fighting for her. I don't really blame you for everything that's happened since we went to the island, Alex. I don't blame you for anything."

His words might have sounded better if they hadn't been delivered in the grim tone of someone who was trying to set the record straight before they died. Was this how we were going to spend our last hours, gong over the things we were sorry for? I couldn't do it. I wasn't going to sit here in this small, hot building and wait to die.

I turned to Sam and said, "Thanks, man," using his standard term of address as I had once done with Mike.

I got up and went over to the monitors, glancing at the images on them. One of the monitors showed a corridor that was in complete darkness. "Where's this?" I asked Tanya.

"Johnny and I found it," she said, coming over and taking a seat next to me. "We were going to show you when you got back, but then…things happened…and I forgot about it. This is a corridor on level two. Remember how all the lights are off on that level? There's only one main room on that level. This camera is in that room. See those shapes in there?"

I studied the blackness on the monitor. There were bulky square-shaped objects lined up in the room.

"What are they?" Jax asked, leaning in closer.

"They're computer servers," Tanya said. "That room houses the servers that run the computer network." She pointed to one of the maps on the desk. "This room here is the server room, and this is the corridor that leads to it." She pointed to another, smaller room on the map. "This is the level 2 maintenance room. It contains the fuse box that runs the electricity on level 2. Johnny thought that one of the fuses must have blown, plunging the entire floor into darkness."

"And cutting power to the servers," I said.

She nodded.

"I turned to Colbert. "You said that your emails and video calls stopped suddenly, so you couldn't contact Alpha One."

"Yes, that's right."

"And those videos you showed us on Vess's computer were stored on his hard drive."

"Yes."

I looked at Tanya. I was sure we were both thinking the same thing. The servers going down had cut all network connections to the outside world. If we restored power to the servers, we might be able to contact Alpha One.

"Do you think it's worth the risk?" I asked her.

She knew exactly what I meant. "Turning those servers back on is probably our only hope of getting Hart's men out here before time runs out."

I brought up other areas of level 2 on the other monitors. The main corridor by the elevator was packed with zombies, visible as shambling shadows in the darkness. I now knew that because the main corridors were accessible from the main stairs by swing doors, the zombies tended to gather in these areas.

"We can get to the servers and the maintenance room via the emergency stairs, and avoid those zombies by the elevators," I said.

"Count me in." Sam got to his feet, his earlier grim mood seemingly gone. "I've always been a sucker for a life or death situation."

"I'll go too," Tanya said. "I'm tired of sitting here not being able to do anything."

I said to Jax, "Could you and Doctor Colbert watch the monitors and help us?"

She nodded. "Of course."

Before we went across the parking lot to the main building, we emptied our backpacks of rations and water, putting those items into the back of the camper van. We also put all of the H1NZ1 into one pack and loaded that into the vehicle. There was no point taking the precious chemical back into the building with us. If we didn't come back out of there, Jax and Doctor Colbert would be back at square one with no chemical.

This way, if we managed to get the servers online but didn't get out alive, Alpha One could be contacted and Jax and the doctor could take the H1NZ1 to the island to save themselves and Lucy.

Tanya and Sam shared the remaining MP5 rounds between themselves so that each rifle was loaded. I took a freshly charged walkie-talkie from the charger in the guard station. I felt like I was in a montage from an eighties TV show where the good guys are getting ready to face the bad guys and prepare themselves while the soundtrack plays a synth-laden piece of inspiring music.

## LIGHTNING

Except this wasn't a movie. Any blood spilled in that building would be real, not fake. And the bad guys weren't actors; they were real-life monsters.

"You ready?" Tanya asked me as I clipped the fresh walkie-talkie to my backpack strap.

I nodded. I was as ready as I was ever going to be.

The three of us walked across the parking lot to the main building. The rain was still hammering down, splashing into puddles that had formed on the parking lot surface and pinging off the cars. Distant thunder rumbled as we reached the main door into the building.

Tanya held her door card ready near the digital lock. She looked at Sam and me. "Let's do this as quickly as we can."

Sam and I nodded.

Tanya opened the door and we stepped inside.

# CHAPTER 16

**S**TEPPING INTO THE QUIET RECEPTION area, I felt a familiar sense of dread in my stomach. It was as if the building itself was a huge monster and we had just willingly stepped into its mouth to be eaten. Nobody in their right mind would come in here unless they were desperate. And that was exactly what we were; those servers on level 2 were our only means of getting back to Apocalypse Island and being injected with the antivirus that would prevent us from losing every last shred of our humanity. I would do anything to see Lucy again, and if that meant entering this monster-infested building once more, then so be it.

But that determination did nothing to quiet my fear.

We crossed the reception area quickly and silently, heading through the access door that led to the emergency stairs. Tanya took the lead, with Sam behind her. I stayed

LIGHTNING

behind them; they had the big guns and were cooler under pressure than I could ever be.

When we got to the emergency stairs, they pushed through the doors quickly. I wanted to tell them that we should check the area ahead before we went charging up the stairs, but they were already ascending the steel steps. They seemed so eager to get this done that they had lost an edge of caution. I followed them at their pace, almost running up the steps to keep up.

We were halfway between level 1 and level 2 when the first hybrid appeared above us. It had once been a woman known as Doctor Debra Francis, according to the name badge on the lapel of its lab coat. Now it was a monster, a killing machine we had to deal with.

It rushed down the stairs toward Sam, lips drawn back and teeth bared. Sam was taken by surprise. He let out a yell and instinctively stepped back to avoid the hybrid. He lost his footing and tripped backward on the stairs, dropping to the unforgiving steel with a grunt of pain.

The hybrid continued past Sam, carried by its momentum, and made a grab for me. It got hold of my shoulder and we tumbled together down the hard steps. I tried to hold it at arm's length because even as we were falling, it tried to sink its teeth into me.

I landed on my back, the hybrid on top of me. It snarled and leaned its face forward, ready to bite. Its breath smelled of rancid meat, probably the remnants of its last meal.

A shot rang out in the stairwell, and the hybrid dropped heavily to one side, blood spurting from its head.

I pushed it off me and stood up quickly. Tanya was crouched in a firing position, the MP5 raised.

"Thanks," I said.

"No problem."

I saw a second hybrid coming down to us, this one a man in a shirt and tie. His yellow eyes were wild and hateful.

"Behind you!" I shouted to Tanya.

She whirled around and fired. The hybrid dropped immediately to avoid the bullet, crawling down the steps toward us like a spider.

Sam had regained his footing. He aimed at the hybrid's head and fired. The hybrid skidded to a halt, blood pouring from its temple.

Walking over to the lifeless body, Sam kicked it with the toe of his boot. "That's some fucked-up shit, man."

We continued up the stairs with more caution. I had a pain across the back of my shoulders where I had slammed into the steps and a throbbing tenderness in my right elbow. If we had been more careful, that could have been avoided. We couldn't afford to get sloppy now, not when so much was at stake.

When we reached the second floor, I asked Jax over the walkie-talkie if the corridor beyond the door was clear.

"All clear," she said, her voice sounding distant through the crackling airwaves. "At least, I think it is. The lights are out, so it's difficult to see."

Tanya opened the door onto the dark corridor. The smell of petrol hit me immediately. It was so strong that it burned my nose.

"Wow," Sam said. "This must be the no-smoking zone." He turned on his flashlight. I did the same, playing my beam along the corridor. Red plastic petrol canisters lay littered all around. The floor and walls seemed to be soaked with the flammable liquid. My flashlight picked up an axe, its head buried deeply in the wall as if someone had swung it with all their might.

"What the hell happened here?" I asked.

Tanya shrugged. We carefully moved farther along the corridor and found two male bodies lying face down. It looked like their spines were gone but the abundance of blood and guts made it difficult to tell for sure.

"Do you think they poured the gas over everything?" Tanya asked.

"It looks like it. Maybe they were trying to kill Vess. If so, their plan must have gone horribly wrong."

We stepped past the dead bodies and found the door marked *Maintenance Room*. Tanya opened the door, stepping back as I shone my flashlight inside.

The room was small, barely more than a cupboard. Wooden shelves were fixed to the walls, holding cleaning equipment, some power tools, and plastic containers full of nails and screws. The fuse box was positioned on the back wall, thick wires running from it into the wall. I inspected the row of switches. All except two were in the up position, indicating that they were on. The two in the down position were labeled *Server Room* and *Light Circuit.*

It was hard to believe that by flicking these switches, we could establish communication with Alpha One and save our own lives. It almost seemed too simple.

I flicked them both to the upward position. The overhead fluorescent lights in the corridor came on, casting stark illumination over the bloody bodies on the floor. "We should check the servers," I said.

We walked quickly to the server room and opened the door. There was a hum in the room. It sounded like everything was booting up. Red, yellow, and green lights began flashing and I could hear the whir of fans within the servers.

Doctor Colbert's voice came over the walkie-talkie. "Bring a laptop. I can try to log onto the network."

"Okay," I said as we went back out into the gasoline-filled corridor.

I opened the door next to the maintenance room, hoping to find an office with a computer, but instead I was looking into a large storeroom with shelves full of chemicals in plastic containers and larger drums on the floor. Everything was labeled as flammable. It seemed a strange place to store such chemicals; I would have

# LIGHTNING

thought that these things would usually be kept in a fireproof room.

Maybe the two dead guys had tried to set a trap for Vess, or the zombies, hoping to burn them. The petrol was all over the floors and walls in here too. Someone had splashed it around everywhere for a purpose, and the only purpose I could see was to blow up these chemicals. Maybe they were trying to make an explosion so big that the sprinkler system wouldn't be able to handle it. Maybe they had realized that they couldn't defeat Vess unless they blew up the entire building.

My guesses were just that...guesses. I couldn't know what had happened here in the madness that had occurred after patient zero had gotten loose in the building. Maybe the two dead guys had simply lost their minds.

"We need to get off this level," I said, "The smell is going to make me puke and we should get a far away from this stuff as possible. We can find a laptop somewhere else."

Tanya and Sam nodded. As we headed back the way we had come, I heard a noise behind us that sent my fear level spiking, the crash of the metal air vent grille hitting the floor. All three of us spun around to face the creature that had once been a scientist but was now a bloodthirsty monster. Vess stood facing us with a sneer on his lips. He knew we couldn't escape him; it was too far to the stairs and he was too fast. He stepped forward, his eyes flicking from Tanya, to Sam, and then to me as if he were deciding which one of us to kill first.

When those yellow eyes met mine, I felt as if Vess could see inside me all the way to my spine.

Adrenaline rushed into my system, making me panic. There was no way we were going to get away from him. I wondered if those dead men had felt the same desperation when they had decided to blow up the building.

Vess took another step forward. I felt like I was frozen to the spot in the floor. Sam grabbed my shoulders and pulled me along the corridor toward the stairs. Tanya was sprinting for the door.

I wanted to tell Sam that there was no point in running; Vess would catch us no matter how fast we ran.

I fished the matches out of my pocket and struck one. It flared to life with a hiss. I couldn't see any way to escape the monster with the yellow eyes that could see right through me other than completing the task the two dead men on the floor had started.

I threw the match. The flame spread immediately. Vess stepped back as the flame ignited the petrol beneath his feet.

I ran for the stairs as fast as I could, not daring to look over my shoulder. Whether Vess came running after us or not, we had to get away from the corridor; once the flames reached the chemicals in the storeroom, there was going to be an almighty explosion.

# LIGHTNING

I was slower than Tanya and Sam, and by the time I got through the door, they were already halfway down to the first floor. I had stumbled down the first two steps when the chemicals erupted. A wave of force and heat knocked me off my feet. I rolled down the steel steps and hit the wall. Staggering to my feet, I saw a bright orange glow beyond what was left of the door. Even the sprinkler system wouldn't be able to douse that fire, and if there were labs on the second floor with more chemicals, things were going to get worse.

Getting to my feet, I followed Tanya and Sam to the first floor. We sprinted across the reception area to the main door as a fire alarm began to wail.

The door slid open when Tanya ran her card through the lock. We went outside into the storm. Tanya and Sam sprinted for the guard station.

When I reached the parking lot, I stopped running and stood with my face turned up to the downpour. The heat wave from the explosion had singed my skin slightly, and the cool night rain had never felt so good against my face.

Sam looked over his shoulder, saw me, then came back to grab me by the shoulders. "We need to get out of here," he shouted as he dragged me toward the camper van.

I nodded, shook off his hands, and staggered through the storm toward the vehicle. My legs felt weak and I was out of breath. The adrenaline rush was gone and now I was crashing.

I could feel the heat of the burning building against my back. Somewhere inside, another explosion sounded, this one ripping out the windows and sending glass crashing into the compound.

Jax and Doctor Colbert appeared outside the guard station, standing in the shaft of light that angled out from the doorway as they watched the building burn. The cars in the parking lot seemed to flicker in the light from the flames.

I reached the camper van and leaned against it, trying to catch my breath as I looked back at the building. Most of the second floor windows were gone, a plume of dirty black smoke rising from them into the night sky. There was an acrid smell in the air, and I wondered if it might be poisonous. Those chemicals were probably dangerous.

"We need to get out of here," Tanya said. Her voice was flat, unemotional. I knew what she was thinking.

If she didn't want to voice her opinion yet, Sam had no problem voicing his. "Way to go, Alex. You just destroyed our last hope of survival, man."

I didn't argue with him; he was right. We had risked our lives to get the servers back online, and I had just panicked and blown them up. Everything on level 2 was burning, and so were our hopes of contacting Site Alpha One.

"We need to leave," Tanya said again. "This place will be crawling with zombies soon." She got into the driver's seat and slammed the door.

# LIGHTNING

I climbed into the rear of the camper van and went all the way to the back of the vehicle, shrugging off my backpack before sitting heavily on the padded bench that served as a sofa. I didn't need to be reminded of how my stupid actions had just cost us our lives. That was surely going to be the hot topic of the evening, so I sat in the darkness alone while the others sat in the front seats.

Sam opened the gate and Tanya drove us out of the compound, waiting on the outside of the fence for Sam to return to the van. When he did so, Tanya put the van into the gear and drove along the track without a word to anyone. Everyone was silent. The only sound was the hum of the engine, the drumming of rain on the van roof, and a distant crackling coming from the burning building behind us.

I looked out through the rear window. Flames and black smoke rose out of the second floor windows. The orange glow in the night sky would be visible to every zombie and hybrid within a twenty-mile radius.

After a few minutes, Tanya turned the van onto a second track that ran through the woods. We bumped along through the trees for a few minutes before she cut the engine. With the vehicle's lights extinguished, we were in total darkness. All I could hear now was the patter of rain on the van and the murmur of my companions as they spoke about what had just happened.

I didn't need to go over it all again. What was the point? With the exception of Doctor Colbert, we were all as good as dead. I wasn't going to talk about it.

Through the window, in the distance, I could just make out the orange flames through a gap in the trees. I leaned back and watched them. They flickered and died over and over in a pattern that was hypnotic.

The monotonous flash of color made my eyelids heavy. I decided to close my eyes and shut out the world. Just for a moment.

# CHAPTER 17

ELTA TWO FIVE, THIS IS Charlie Ten. Do you have eyes on the location? Over." The voice that cut through the darkness in my mind was unfamiliar, so I knew I must have been dreaming it. I tried to ignore it so I could sleep some more.

I heard a crackle of static, then a second voice. "Charlie Ten, this is Delta Two Five. Affirmative. We have a number of tangos inside the perimeter fence. Dealing with the situation now. Over."

I heard gunshots in the distance. Opening my eyes, I realized it was light outside. The pale morning sunlight cast a flat, cool light over the woods. Mist clung to the ground in sinuous tendrils. I sat up and rubbed my eyes before checking my watch. The countdown timer showed 16:03. Only sixteen hours left to live.

I thought I had dreamed the gunshots, but I heard them again. My walkie-talkie, still clipped to my backpack, crackled. "Tango down."

I sat up on the sofa. Sam was sprawled out on the floor, covered with a blanket he must have found in the van. Tanya and Jax were in the driver and passenger seats, also under blankets, and Colbert was lying on the rear seat behind them. As I got up from the sofa, they began to stir.

I went to the side window and looked out, pressing my forehead against the cold glass. Last night's storm had passed. Through the mist and trees, I could just make out the road that led to Alpha Two. Trucks and personnel carriers were rolling along that road, all painted in drab olive green.

I grabbed the walkie-talkie and turned up the volume.

"Delta Two Five, this is Charlie Ten. We are setting up a perimeter around the location. What's the situation there? Over."

Sam sat up quickly. "What the fuck is that?"

"The army is here," I said. "They must have seen the fire."

"That's all we need, man, the fucking army. What time is it?"

"Six thirty."

He got up and stretched, moving over to the window to watch the trucks on the road. Tanya, Jax, and Colbert were also awake, and listening to the conversation coming from the walkie-talkie.

"Charlie Ten, we have a number of tangos around the building. We're dealing with them now." When Delta Two Five spoke, he had to shout to be heard over gunfire. A few seconds after his message had ended, the sound of that gunfire reached the camper van.

I heard a chopper overhead, then the message, "Delta Two Five, the bird is on its way to your location."

"What are they doing here?" Colbert asked.

I shrugged. "The fire must have attracted their attention. They'd probably already known about site Alpha Two but left it alone. Last night, they must have seen the explosion. It lit up the sky for miles around. A fire at a government facility is something that interests them, I suppose."

"Charlie Ten, copy that. We'll wait for the breathing equipment before entering the building. We have a visual on the bird, and have marked a landing area within the compound. Tell the pilot to look for the flares located south of the building. Over."

"Affirmative, Delta Two Five."

"They're going inside," Jax said.

I nodded. "Big mistake. If Vess is still alive, they might as well ring a dinner bell before they go in."

"He's alive," Sam said. "Alex's stupid stunt might have wiped out most of the building, but Vess is still in there."

"He was going to kill us," I said. "I panicked."

"We're dead anyway, man." He stared out of the window at the misty woods.

I cleared my throat. "That's something we need to discuss. What's going to happen tonight when we turn? I don't know about any of you, but I don't want to become a monster." I looked at Doctor Colbert. "I'll give you my gun later. When the time comes, will you do the right thing?"

She nodded grimly.

"Hart should be here tomorrow," I told her. "Try and get the H1NZ1 to him."

"Do you think he's going to land here with the army crawling all over everything?" Sam asked.

"I don't know," I said, "but we have to hope he will. He was willing to risk it when he thought the area might be full of zombies."

"Zombies don't have guns."

"I don't think the army will shoot at a helicopter from Site Alpha One," Doctor Colbert said. "I'll make sure he gets the H1NZ1."

"Thanks," I said. At least Lucy would be okay. Our mission to Alpha Two hadn't been totally in vain.

The walkie-talkie crackled. "Charlie One, we've unloaded the breathing equipment from the bird. I'm sending a recon team of six men into the building now."

"Affirmative, Delta Two Five."

If Vess was still in there, those six soldiers were being sent to their deaths. I remembered how Vess had killed Johnny, tearing out his spine cruelly. I hoped the fire had

LIGHTNING

destroyed Vess but, like Sam, I was sure that he was still alive.

A new voice came over the static. "This is Recon One. We are at the front entrance, standing by."

Delta Two Five said, "Recon One, standby." Then, a moment later, "Go."

I heard a sound like a small explosion come over the airwaves, and then the recon team leader said, "Go, go, go." It sounded like he had taped down the button on his walkie-talkie to give Delta Two Five a running commentary as they searched the building. I assumed the explosion I had heard was some sort of charge they had detonated to blow the main door.

A voice shouted, "Clear!"

"Reception area clear," Recon One's leader said. "Advancing to stairs."

"Where are they going?" Colbert asked.

"Probably the second floor," Tanya said. "They probably want to know what caused that explosion."

"I can tell them that," Sam said, pointing at me. "He's right here."

"Tangos on stairs. Engaging." Bursts of gunfire and shouts of, "Tango down!" came over the static. The shouts sounded muffled by the breathing equipment the soldiers were wearing. It was about a minute before the firing stopped. A steady voice said, "Stairway clear. Proceeding."

"It didn't take them long to deal with those nasties on the stairs," Sam said.

143

I nodded. "But now they've given away their location with all that noise. If Vess is still alive, he'll be there in a heartbeat."

"If he's still alive," Sam said, "blowing up the building was fucking pointless."

"Entering level two," Recon One's leader said calmly. "Engaging tangos." More gunfire erupted. We had seen a lot of zombies by the level two elevators, which was where the recon team would be standing now, but the zombies had probably moved when the fire started and the sprinklers kicked in.

It only took thirty seconds before we heard someone shout, "Clear!"

"Proceeding to east side of building," the leader said. Then, "Holding position. What was that noise?"

A soldier said something I couldn't hear.

"Check it out," the leader said. Then into the walkie-talkie, he reported, "Investigating noise in air vent."

Shouts and gunfire broke through the static. "Man down!" the leader shouted. "What the fuck was that?"

More shouts, more gunfire. "Fall back to stairs! It's got Samuels! Oh, my God!" More shots were fired. I heard a man scream.

"It took his spine," the leader said in disbelief. His breathing sounded loud and close, even over the poor reception of the walkie-talkie. "Fall back!"

Another scream was followed by more shots. "Fuck!" Recon One's leader breathed.

"It's too fast," a soldier shouted before he began screaming.

"Falling back," the leader whispered. "They've all gone. It took my men." I could hear his labored breathing as he fled down the stairs, then a low growl coming from somewhere close to him.

The last thing the Recon One leader said was, "No! Please!"

Then there was nothing more but the hiss of static.

I looked at the others. Colbert's face had gone pale, her eyes fixed on the walkie-talkie. Tanya's eyes held their usual cold look, and I wondered if she was thinking that blowing up the servers had not only killed us, but also these soldiers. They probably wouldn't be here if not for the explosion. Jax was sitting quietly, her eyes bloodshot. I wondered if she still felt ill.

Sam looked at me and raised his eyebrow. "Well done, dude, you just killed six soldiers without even leaving the comfort of the van."

"Leave him alone," Jax said. "Alex did what he thought was best at the time. He couldn't have known the army was going to come here and go into the building."

"Thanks, Jax," I said to her.

"It doesn't matter. What's done is done. I need some air." Tanya went to the side door of the van and opened it. She stepped outside.

"I need to stretch my legs," I said. At that moment, I needed to be as far away from the others as possible. I couldn't take any more of their accusing glances, especially not today.

The morning was cold and damp, the woods smelling strongly of pine and earth. I walked past Tanya and into the woods, away from the road.

"Be careful, Alex," she said,

I nodded but said nothing. It didn't really matter if I was careful or not. My fate was sealed, and so was hers.

I walked aimlessly for a while, listening to the birds singing in the trees, feeling the cool breeze on my face, and wondering how things could have turned out differently if Doctor Marcus Vess hadn't decided to prove that his serum was harmless by injecting it into himself. The smallest event could trigger a catastrophe. The human race could be brought to its knees by something as simple as a microscopic virus.

I found a fallen, mossy tree stump and sat down for a while, watching the sun come up over the trees and burn off the mist. If this was to be my last day on Earth, at least I was in a beautiful setting. Things could be worse. At least I wasn't spending my last few hours in a Survivors Camp as so many people had. I closed my eyes and listened to the birdsong.

The serenity of the moment was killed when I heard someone shout, "Get out of the vehicle!"

Moving quickly back the way I had come, I stayed low as I approached the camper van. What I saw made my heart sink.

LIGHTNING

At least a dozen soldiers surrounded the van, rifles aimed at Sam, Tanya, Jax, and Doctor Colbert. My friends had their hands up and offered no resistance as the soldiers herded them along the track toward the road where a truck waited.

I heard someone say, "What have we got here, then?"

"Survivors," came a reply. "Fuck knows how they lasted this long."

My friends climbed into the back of the truck at gunpoint. A soldier closed the tailgate, and the truck drove away toward Site Alpha Two.

I waited a few minutes to make sure the area was clear. It was possible that the soldiers might leave a guard her to watch the camper van, but the more I thought about that, the more unlikely it seemed. It would probably be foolish to leave a couple of men in a wood full of zombies. And why bother guarding an empty vehicle? They were securing this whole area, so they could return to the camper van whenever they wanted. It wasn't going anywhere.

I crept into the clearing, pausing every couple of seconds to listen for a sound that might tell me my theory about a guard was wrong. By the time I reached the camper van, I was sure I was alone here.

I opened the side door and went into the vehicle. The soldiers had taken the weapons and some of the equipment we had brought with us but they had left a backpack of rations, and the pack that contained the H1NZ1. They had missed it in their hasty search, not understood what it was, or decided to come back later to search the vehicle properly.

I slung the pack onto my back and adjusted the straps so that it fit comfortably. I wasn't sure why I was taking it with me but I couldn't abandon the thing we had worked so hard to obtain. There might be some way I could get it to Doctor Colbert, and I was going to try my best to do that.

Besides, Johnny Drake had died for this chemical so I wasn't going to just leave it here.

# CHAPTER 18

STAYED AWAY FROM THE road as I crept through the woods toward the facility. I had the Desert Eagle in my hand, but there was no way I was going to get into a shootout with soldiers. I refused to shoot at living human beings. Also, I had hardly ever shot a gun, and I was sure to be killed instantly if I went up against men who were highly trained in the use of firearms.

I had no idea what I was going to do once I found out where they were holding my friends, other than try to liberate them from the army's clutches.

Luckily, I met no resistance, and soon reached an area at the edge of the woods where I could observe the facility and remain out of sight, staying low and close to the tree trunks and undergrowth.

The military had built a camp within the perimeter fence of Site Alpha Two. Dozens of green tents huddled together in the compound. The parking lot was full of army trucks and Land Rovers. There were soldiers scurrying everywhere. As I watched, a Chinook helicopter descended onto a flat area of grass, the ramp at the rear lowering to allow even more personnel into the camp. After a few moments, the Chinook took off again, presumably to fetch even more personnel. It whirred away over the distant hills and out of sight.

The compound, which had been quiet yesterday when we'd arrived, was buzzing with noise and an atmosphere of expectancy. The fire in the building seemed to have died out. Black soot covered the outer walls above the second floor windows and a foul smell of burnt rubber and plastic hung in the air, but I couldn't see any flames or smoke.

Teams of soldiers were being shown floor plans of the building on a large screen, the areas of interest pointed out by a large man wearing a maroon beret. I couldn't believe they were going to send more people in there after what had happened to Recon One.

Somewhere, in one of the tents, Sam, Tanya, Jax, and Doctor Colbert were probably being questioned. Maybe they could warn the soldiers not to go into the building, tell them about Vess. I laughed at that thought. Would the men in charge listen? I already knew the answer to that.

There seemed to be nothing I could do to help my friends. If I tried to get into the compound, I was going to be caught. That wouldn't help anyone.

I sat back against a tree trunk and checked my watch. Did any of this even matter when we had less than fourteen hours left to live? If Tanya, Sam, and Jax turned while being held in the camp, the soldiers were going to be sorry. I doubted that there would be anyone left alive in there by morning.

Was there anything I could do other than sit here and wait? It felt wrong to spend my last few hours sitting alone in these woods while my friends spent theirs as prisoners of the army.

I studied the compound again. Guards were posted at the gate and in the security-guard station that we had occupied earlier. I wondered if they were using the camera monitors to explore the interior of the building just as we had. How would things be different in there now that most of level 2 had gone up in smoke? The zombies in the stairwell had probably been driven up to higher levels or down to level 1. Probably both.

And where was Vess? Was he still roaming the air vents or had he found refuge elsewhere? One thing was certain; with the army sending more men inside, Vess was going to have plenty of prey to hunt down and tear apart.

The military presence seemed to be concentrated at the front of the building, the grassy area at the rear being deserted. With the amount of men they were flying in, they would probably have to extend the camp to that area too, eventually, but for now it was still empty of soldiers.

If I could get over the fence around the back, I wouldn't have to worry about the guards at the gate. I'd have a good chance of getting into the compound undiscovered. But what would I do once I was in there? I couldn't go knocking on every tent, asking if anyone had seen my friends.

I put the Desert Eagle in its holster. I had no ideas left. We had done well to get the H1NZ1 but in the end, a superior force had overwhelmed us. We couldn't fight against the army.

My journey since the first day of the zombie breakout had been a harrowing one. I'd avoided army patrols, escaped from a zombie-infested lighthouse, been part of a mission to the Survivor Radio studios, and entered a secret government site to extract a chemical that would be used to create an antivirus.

And I'd fallen in love. My biggest regret about ending my journey here, among these trees, was that I wasn't with Lucy. But I was still thankful that I had at least met Lucy and spent precious time with her, even if I couldn't be with her at the end.

I looked down at the Desert Eagle in its holster. Should I just blow my brains out now? If I waited until I was about to turn, I might not have the will to do it. I had no idea what signs to look for that would mean I was on the verge of turning. And by the time I recognized them, it might be too late, my brain already under the control of the virus.

LIGHTNING

The army would probably kill me eventually but how many innocent people would I tear apart before they managed to catch me?

I sat staring at the trees around me, letting my thoughts zone out. When I checked my watch later, the countdown told me that I had been sitting there for over an hour.

I was wasting precious time. If I was going to end this on my own terms, then I needed to get on with it.

A distant sound caught my attention. Standing up to stretch my aching muscles, I saw the Chinook coming over the hills, probably bringing more personnel to the camp.

As I watched the chopper's approach, a shout went up near the building.

Recon One had blown the main door off its hinges when they had gone inside earlier but no one had thought to seal the doorway afterward, and now dozens of zombies were shambling out into the camp, attracted by the noise and movement.

Shots rang out as soldiers began firing on the creatures. As zombies fell by the doorway, others stepped over their bodies, arms outstretched as they lurched toward the soldiers, their hungry moans filling the air.

Chaos reigned as soldiers and zombies went to war The soldiers were in possession of enough firepower to take over a small nation, but the zombies were among them, making it difficult for them to shoot without hitting other soldiers. The large number of personnel in the camp was a drawback when it came to fighting at such close quarters.

Some of the soldiers, seeing the futility of fighting a large number of zombies when they were unable to fire for fear of hitting their comrades, ran for the gate. Others tried to use their weapons as clubs. Some must have thought it better to risk shooting a fellow soldier if it meant they had a chance to kill a zombie and they fired their rifles. Soldiers and zombies dropped to the ground as shots rang out in the morning air.

The Chinook had reached the compound. It hovered uncertainly above the fence for a moment before flying to the grassy area at the back of the building, the pilot obviously deciding it was safer to land there. As it descended, I broke cover and ran for the gate, seeing an opportunity to get into the compound. The guards who had been stationed at the gate were running toward the melee in the camp to help their comrades, their posts abandoned.

Sprinting past the security guard station and across the parking lot toward the grounded Chinook, I saw the rear ramp descend to drop off a group of soldiers. They ran around to the front of the building to enter the battle raging there.

I crouched behind a blue Nova while they passed me. Their attention was focused on the chaos in front of them. No one even glanced in my direction.

# LIGHTNING

As the last soldier ran past, I sprinted for the rear of the Chinook, taking the Desert Eagle from its holster. When I got to the top of the ramp, I ran up to the open doorway that separated the cockpit from the rear of the helicopter and leaned through, pressing the muzzle of my gun against the pilot's helmet.

"Get us in the air," I said.

The co-pilot looked at me with a look of astonishment.

"Do it," I said, "or I'll blow his fucking brains out."

"Okay, okay."

They both began to flick switches on the control panel. The rear ramp lifted up and closed.

"Get us up!" I demanded.

They complied, taking the Chinook up until it was above the height of the building.

"Now what?" the pilot asked. "What do you want us to do?"

"I want you to do exactly as I say. We're going to pick up some precious cargo."

# CHAPTER 19

TOLD THEM TO TAKE us over the building to where the fight was raging. The situation on the ground had gotten worse. Bodies of soldiers and zombies were strewn everywhere. It was obvious that some of the soldiers had been shot by their colleagues, their blood staining the grass around them.

The ones that had been bitten were staggering toward the gate and into the woods, muttering the words, "Leave me alone" as the virus combined with the vaccine in their blood and compelled them to seek a quiet place to turn into hybrids.

Still more zombies were coming out of the building. There was such chaos in the camp that the creatures were able to get outside through the doorway without even being shot at.

LIGHTNING

In the mass of olive-green uniforms and white lab coats, it was easy to spot Sam, Jax, Tanya, and Doctor Colbert. They were fleeing the fight, heading for the gate.

"See those people?" I said to the pilot, the Desert Eagle still pointed at his head. "We're going to go down there and pick them up."

He shook his head. "There's nowhere to land down there."

I pointed at a small area near the parking lot. If we got there quickly enough, we would be there before my friends made it out of the gate. "There," I said. "Land there."

"There are zombies everywhere," the co-pilot protested.

"We only need a few seconds," I said. "Now do it, or I will shoot both of you. Believe me, I've got nothing to lose."

They must have detected the desperation in my voice, because they took the Chinook down to the exact spot I had indicated.

The helicopter's side door was located just behind the cockpit, so I could open it while still keeping the pilot in my sights. I was never going to shoot him or the co-pilot, but they didn't know that, and I probably seemed crazy to them, which was enough to make them comply.

I opened the door and shouted, "Sam! Tanya!"

They saw me and changed the trajectory of their run, heading for the helicopter at full speed.

157

A zombie that had been in the area when we landed came around the side of the Chinook, moaning at me, his arms outstretched. I used the Desert Eagle to dispatch him, aiming between his eyes and pulling the trigger. The gun recoiled in my hand like a striking snake. The zombie fell to the ground and lay there, unmoving.

The sound of the gun spooked the pilot. He began to lift us back into the air. I whirled on him, pointing the gun at his face. "Don't you fucking take off until I tell you."

He removed his hands from the controls as if they were suddenly hot. "Okay, just stay calm."

I noticed two hybrids break from the pack of shambling zombies and begin to chase Doctor Colbert and Jax. Doctor Colbert was the slowest runner, and Jax was hanging back to encourage her to move faster.

The hybrids were both ex-security guards at the facility, dressed in dark uniform, but both without their caps. They had once been a dark-haired woman, and a bald man with a moustache and beard. Now, they were monsters. They fixed on Doctor Colbert like a pair of lions selecting the slowest gazelle from the pack.

I knew there was no point in shouting at Doctor Colbert to run faster; she already looked like she was about to collapse. She was sucking in air like crazy, her face red and sweaty. Her legs were weak and unable to keep the pace Jax had set.

# LIGHTNING

Tanya reached the Chinook and ran in through the door, closely followed by Sam. "Watch the pilots," I said. "Don't let them take us up."

I ran out of the chopper, the Desert Eagle in both hands like I had seen on cop shows. But I was no cop, and this wasn't television. I didn't dare fire while Jax and Doctor Colbert were in the way.

But if I didn't shoot, the hybrids would definitely catch them. Even now, they were only ten feet behind their prey. "Get down!" I shouted.

Jax looked at me as if I had gone crazy. She knew they were being chased, so why would they stop?

"Trust me and get down," I said, trying to hold the gun steady.

For a moment, I thought Jax was going to ignore me and keep on running, only to be brought down by the hybrids. But she must have decided to trust me because she grabbed Doctor Colbert and pulled her to the ground. Unable to slow their momentum, they crashed and rolled in the dirt.

I fired my first shot, hitting the bearded hybrid in the chest. Unlike zombies, hybrids were alive, so a shot that could kill a living person would kill a hybrid. The bullet stopped this one dead in its tracks.

Jerking the gun sights to aim at the other hybrid, I pulled the trigger just as the creature reached Doctor Colbert. Its head was flung back as the bullet tore into its skull.

Jax scrambled to her feet, pulling a huffing and puffing Doctor Colbert along by her arm. When they reached me, Jax whispered, "Thank you."

We got on board the Chinook and I told the pilot to take off.

"Where are we going?" he asked.

I grinned. "Have you ever heard of a place called Apocalypse Island?"

"No." He looked at me as if I had asked him to fly us to Middle Earth.

"It's not on your maps," Sam said. "I'll give you the coordinates." As he stepped past me to talk to the pilots, he put a hand on my shoulder. "Good work, man."

I nodded and went back to the seating area where the others were recovering from their ordeal.

"I knew you'd come for us," Tanya said. "Even though we only had a few hours left, I knew you'd try to rescue us."

"It's like Sam said in the lab," Jax said, "You're an optimist, Alex. You don't give up."

I didn't mention the fact that I had been about to take my own life when I had seen an opportunity to get into the compound and seized it. Maybe I would never tell anyone that, not even Lucy.

I took a seat next to Jax and said, "Thanks for trusting me."

She smiled. "Thanks for saving my life."

LIGHTNING

Her face was drawn into a grimace of pain, the skin beneath her eyes dark and blotchy.

"Are you okay?" I asked her.

She nodded and gave me a tight-lipped smile. "I will be. Once I get the antivirus. The stomach pain is still there, and I've been having... strange thoughts."

"Strange thoughts?"

"It doesn't matter," she said. "We're on our way back to the island. Everything will be fine."

I smiled at her but I wasn't going to relax until we'd all been injected with the antivirus. My optimism only went so far.

Only when the antivirus was pumping through our veins would this nightmare be over.

# CHAPTER 20

APOCALYPSE ISLAND LOOKED DIFFERENT FROM the air. I had gone up to the cockpit, impatient to get to the island, and unable to sit on the seats because I was full of adrenaline. Through the windshield, I saw the island, sitting solidly in a rough sea beneath the sun.

When we had approached it in the boats, it had seemed a dangerous place, surrounded by lethal spurs of rock that would tear up any boat that came too close. The cliffs had looked daunting and impenetrable.

From the air, Apocalypse Island looked neat and green, the woods covering almost the entire area except for the central grassland where Site Alpha One stood. From up here, you would never guess that zombies and hybrids lurked in those woods.

Sam pointed out the area where the two Chinooks sat by the hangar. One of those choppers was supposed to come and collect us from Site Alpha Two tomorrow. It would have been much too late by then.

"Take her down over there, man," Sam told the pilot.

We descended gently, the rotors kicking up dust and flattening the surrounding grass as the pilot took us down. I opened the side door. Doctor Colbert and Jax climbed out, followed by Tanya and myself. I heard Sam say to the pilot, "Remember, man, this place doesn't exist. You were never here," before he climbed out to join us.

The Chinook took to the sky, turned toward the mainland, and flew out of sight. I wondered what the pilot and co-pilot were going to tell their superiors when they returned. I was sure they'd come up with a plausible story that didn't involve being hijacked and forced to fly to a secret island.

The hangar door opened and Hart came walking out with a handful of his men. He didn't seem surprised to see us at all. He had told me before we'd left here that he thought we were resourceful. Our presence here now simply proved him right.

"Alex," he said, standing with his hands on his hips. "You're early."

"We have the H1N21," I said, handing him the backpack. "The scientists need to work on the antivirus right now. We don't have much time."

Doctor Colbert stepped forward and explained that we only had a few hours left. She volunteered to help the scientists, some of whom she knew, to produce the antivirus.

"You'll have to be isolated," Hart told us. "It's purely a precaution. Now that we know the real speed at which the pure virus works, we can't take any chances. We'll have the antivirus ready in an hour, so you won't be waiting long."

We were taken to the rooms downstairs and locked in. I paced around my room, but I didn't feel anywhere near the level of anxiety I had felt the last time I was in here. Then, I had thought that I had nothing more than a slim chance of saving Lucy. Now, she was hours away from a cure.

I sat in one of the chairs and folded my arms, letting my chin rest on my chest as I closed my eyes. I was tired. Stress had built up inside me over the past couple of days and now that I had a chance to relax, my mind and body seized that opportunity by making me sleepy. My eyelids felt too heavy to keep open. My arms and legs felt as if they were made of lead and moving them was too much effort. The sound of my own heavy breathing and footsteps in the corridor outside the door were all I could hear, and those sounds seemed to fade into the distance as I fell asleep.

\*\*\*

A loud clanging alarm woke me. I opened my eyes and pushed the chair back from the table. Through the panel of frosted glass in the door, I could see shadows of people running in the corridor, their boots drumming on the floor.

The door burst open suddenly, and three guards came in with rifles leveled at me.

Surprised, I raised my hands. "What's going on?"

Hart entered the room, accompanied by the same scientist who had injected me with the pure virus.

"He looks okay, sir," one of the guards said.

"Yes, I can see that," Hart replied tersely. He looked angry and drained.

"What's happening?" I asked him. Outside the door, guards were still running along the corridor, weapons in their hands.

"Sit down," he said, "We need to inject you immediately."

The scientist came forward with a syringe of clear liquid. I sat in the chair while he injected me. The needle stung as it pierced the skin of my shoulder at the same spot where they had injected me with the virus.

"You're now fully vaccinated," Hart said, waving the others out of the room. "That antivirus will combine with the vaccine in your blood and halt the transformation you would have gone through. You can't be turned now, no matter what happens. If you ever get bitten, you need not fear about turning into a monster."

"What about Lucy?" I asked.

"She'll be fine. We've administered the antivirus. It's just a matter of time before she regains consciousness and awareness. It's the same for Kate, my wife. I owe you a great deal of thanks, Alex."

"What's happening out there?" I asked, pointing to the corridor beyond the door.

He paused for a beat before telling me, "I'm afraid we didn't get the antivirus to one of your friends in time. For some reason, she reacted to the pure strain of the virus faster than the rest of you."

"Jax," I said.

"Yes," Hart said.

"What happened?"

"She's killed three of my men," he said. "Ripped out their spines. And she's escaped the facility. We have teams out in the woods hunting her down."

I couldn't believe it. My brain could hardly comprehend that Jax was a monster like Vess. This had to be a mistake. Surely Jax must be sitting in a room just like this one farther along the corridor. Something else had killed those men. Not Jax.

"I know it's a lot to take in," Hart said, probably guessing my thoughts from the look of disbelief that must be on my face. "I'll leave you alone for a while so you can come to terms with it."

"No," I said. I couldn't bear to be left alone any longer. "I want to see Lucy. Right now."

# CHAPTER 21

I SPENT THE NEXT FOUR hours sitting at Lucy's bedside in the hospital room, watching her gradually awaken. The first thing that changed was her position. She had been curled up in the fetal position when I'd first entered the room, but she gradually straightened her body beneath the covers. Her breathing, which had been ragged, slowed to a normal pace. By the third hour, she looked as if she was simply lying there taking a nap. There were no outward signs of the battle raging inside her body between the virus and the antivirus.

While I waited for Lucy to wake up, I thought about Jax. In the short time I had known her, she had been a good friend. We had talked about the world before the apocalypse, and she had told me about her fears for her boyfriend's safety. She had shown me the engagement ring he had given her, and told me that she regretted not

167

accepting his proposal. Her experience had highlighted a simple truth for me: time is precious.

Now, Jax's time was done. She had become a monster, and all of the thoughts, hopes, and dreams that made Jax the person she was were gone. If Hart's men found her in the woods and killed her, they would be doing her a favor; Jax had never wanted to be a monster. The old Jax, the woman I had spent time with, would be appalled if she knew she would murder at least three innocent people someday, ripping out their spines as Vess had done to Johnny.

I wondered how Sam and Tanya were taking the news of Jax's transformation into a monster and escape into the woods. They had known her for a long time. I guessed it was hitting them hard.

Lucy opened her eyes and blinked at the overhead lights. She turned her head slowly to face me. "Alex?"

I grinned at her and nodded, unable to speak because I knew that if I did, I would start to cry. While sitting here waiting, I had feared that when Lucy finally opened her eyes, they would be yellow zombie eyes, staring at me with malevolence. I had been afraid that the antivirus might not work. But her eyes were the same clear blue they had always been. I let out a sigh of relief.

"You saved me," she whispered.

I spread my hands. "I can't deny it."

She laughed and tried to sit up. But the effort was too much for her, so she sank back down onto the pillows.

LIGHTNING

"Take it easy," I said. "The doctors say it will take a few days to recover fully. You've been through a lot."

"Not really. I've just been sleeping." She looked closely at my face. "But you've been through a lot. I can tell by looking at you."

"Do I really look that bad?"

She shook her head. "It's not that. You look...stronger somehow. But as if you had to go through a lot to gain that strength."

I shrugged. Nobody could be a survivor in a zombie apocalypse and not be changed in some way.

Lucy looked around the room. "Alex, where are we?"

"Apocalypse Island," I said.

She frowned with confusion. "Where?"

I laughed. "I'll tell you all about it later. In fact, I'll write it all down in a journal like I did before."

Lucy nodded, her blue eyes wandering around the room.

"So I just have one question," I said.

She nodded. "I know what it is. Why did I leave you at the marina?"

"Yeah, that's the one."

"After you went ashore, I refueled the boat and waited on the jetty. It was so foggy I couldn't see anything but I could hear sounds all around the marina, splashes and voices. I had no idea how long you were going to be but I felt nervous and vulnerable standing there on the jetty in the fog.

"You said you were going to get a rowboat, so I untied *The Big Easy* and took her out into deeper water. I didn't want anyone running out of that fog and boarding her and since you were getting a rowboat anyway, it wouldn't be a problem for you to row a few more feet to reach the *Easy*. I was no more than twenty feet from the end of the jetty."

"That sounds sensible," I said. I had told Lucy at the time that I was going to find a rowboat but when I was trying to get a boat into the water, feral survivors had attacked me and that was when I discovered that Lucy was gone.

Lucy nodded. "I stood on the deck watching the marina for any movement but the fog was too thick so I listened for the sound of oars in the water. I didn't think you'd be gone for so long."

"I had some trouble," I said. "I heard voices and had to hide in the marine shop for a while."

"When you didn't come back, I started to get even more worried. I wondered what I was going to do if you never came back. How long could I wait here? Once the fog lifted, *The Big Easy* would be visible to the soldiers in the area. I would have to go out deeper and use the binoculars to watch the marina." She looked into my eyes. "I was never going to abandon you, Alex."

"I know that." I took her hand in mine. "I was worried that you'd been captured by the army or attacked by pirates. I had no idea how to find you."

"I decided to move out into deeper water so I started the engine and sailed out to a spot where I could drop anchor and wait. But then I heard another boat approaching. I panicked. I had to get out of there. Before I could get moving, an army boat came out of the fog and drew up alongside the *Easy*. It was a small boat, probably quite fast, and it was painted army green. There were eight soldiers onboard and they were all pointing their guns at me.

"I didn't have time to think what to do. Three of the soldiers came onboard and ordered me off the bridge. I was led at gunpoint to the aft deck and told to stay there. One of the soldiers, a woman named Meyers, sat with me while the other two took control of the *Easy* and followed the army boat along the coast.

"I asked Meyers what was going on and she told me they were going to send me to a Survivors Camp where I'd be safe. I just kept wondering what was going to happen when you returned to find that I was gone. I started to formulate a plan of escape. I even considered jumping overboard but we were in very deep water by now and even if I made it to shore, my chances of getting back to Swansea without any weapons were slim. So I decided to sit tight until a better opportunity presented itself.

"We must have been sailing for about an hour when they cut the engine, dropped anchor, and transferred me to the smaller green boat. The fog had lifted now and I could see a marina that looked like it had been taken over by the army. All the boats moored there were painted in military green. The civilian boats that must have previously used the marina had been anchored in deeper water, where the *Easy* was now anchored.

"They took me ashore and made me wait in a tent while they tried to find out when the next camp truck was passing this way. It sounded like they had trucks travelling around each military camp tasked with picking up survivors to take to the Survivors Camps. Someone said that there was a truck delivering "the vaccine" to the nearest Survivors Camp, so I could ride along. They bundled me into the back of an army truck, one of the ones with a canvas top. There were stacks of cardboard boxes in there, which I assumed held the vaccine the soldiers had been talking about.

"Meyer got into the back with me and sat by the tailgate, watching the landscape roll by as we drove along a country road. I asked her what the soldiers had meant when they'd said the truck was delivering a vaccine. Was there now a vaccine against being bitten? She said there was, and it was being delivered to all the soldiers.

"I told her that I thought that was unfair. Why not give the vaccine to everyone? She just shrugged and continued looking out at the fields and trees. Meyer's lack of concern for civilians made me angry, and my anger spurred me into trying to escape. I could easily jump over the tailgate onto the road. If I ran fast enough, I should be able to reach the woods before they managed to shoot me.

"But before I left the truck, I wanted to get some of the vaccine from the boxes. I thought about just grabbing a box and running with it but they were too big for that so I tore a hole in a box and took a handful of syringes out. They were full of an amber liquid and the needles had plastic caps over them for safety.

"Meyer saw me and came over, demanding that I put the syringes back. She raised her gun and I swatted it out of the way. She fired but the bullets went up through the canvas roof. I ran for the tailgate and swung myself over it.

"When I hit the road, the air was knocked out of my lungs and I dropped all but one of the syringes. I was okay apart from a few scratches but I didn't have time to pick up the syringes of vaccine I'd dropped.

"The driver must have heard the shots because the truck came to a stop. I ran for the woods. They fired a few shots at me but I made it into the trees without being hit. They didn't follow me.

"I found a heavy branch that I could use as a weapon if I ran into any zombies in the woods. I put the syringe into my pocket and followed the direction of the road back to the army marina. I needed to get back onboard *The Big Easy* and sail back to Swansea to find you.

"When I got to the marina, there was a heated discussion going in one of the tents. Apparently, the vaccine was faulty. It stopped someone from becoming a zombie but only for four days. After that, they became something much worse. After hearing that, I decided not to vaccinate myself as I had planned to do when I got back to the *Easy*. If it was faulty, what was the point?

"So I moved along the coast, sticking to the trees, until I found a small rowboat. I waited until nightfall and then I rowed out to where they had anchored the *Easy*. I got the engines started and sailed out of there unchallenged. It seemed the army were using all their resources to guard the marina from inland attacks by zombies and they weren't watching the water at all.

"I got back to Swansea but there was no sign of you. I spent a couple of days watching the marina through the binoculars, making sure I was in deep enough water that I could make a run for it if I saw any army boats. I put the vaccine syringe on a shelf in the storeroom, thinking we'd never need it since it was faulty, but hanging onto it anyway, just in case.

"I sailed north along the coast, scanning the beaches with the binoculars in the hopes of finding you. Eventually, I didn't know what else to do so I did nothing. I just waited on the waves, hoping that somehow you'd find me.

"Then, one evening, I was listening to the radio and I heard someone talking about the zombies only being here in Britain. They said survivors should sail to mainland Europe. And then I heard your voice. I could hardly believe it. I had to pinch myself to make sure I wasn't dreaming. You told me to meet you at the lighthouse in

# LIGHTNING

three days' time so I sailed south of that area. I didn't want to wait for you there...I still hate that place."

I squeezed her hand. "Me too," I said.

"What happened next was a really stupid move on my part," she said. "I waited for two days just south of the lighthouse near a village. I watched the village through the binoculars and the place seemed deserted. No people, no zombies...nothing. I assumed the army had cleared the place and taken all the villagers to a Survivors Camp. Every time I looked through the binoculars over those two days, there was no sign of life, and no sign of danger. Something there kept drawing my attention, though; a village store. It was sitting on the main street within easy reach of the little village harbor.

"And I got a crazy thought in my head. I was so looking forward to being reunited with you that I became fixated on the idea of getting a nice bottle of red wine from that store so that we could celebrate. That thought grew in my head until I couldn't get rid of it. And it looked like there would be no risk in going to the village store.

"So, on the day we were supposed to meet, I decided to swim ashore and get a bottle of wine. I know it sounds crazy, but the next thing I knew, I was taking the *Easy* in to the little harbor. When she was moored, I took a baseball bat just in case and walked up the steep road that led to the main street.

"The shop was unlocked, so I went inside. There was a foul smell in there but I wasn't sure if it was meat products that had gone bad or the smell of a zombie. I went quickly to the wine and selected a bottle. Why I didn't take an armful I don't know, but my mind had become fixated on the idea of one bottle of red wine so that was all I took.

"When I turned to go back to the door, I was attacked. I don't know how it had moved so quietly but there was a zombie right in front of me. I think it had been the shopkeeper. He lunged as I was fumbling with my bat. I managed to shove the bat between his legs, tripping him, but as he went down he bit my right thigh. I'd never felt any pain like it. I cried out and brought the bat down on his skull. Without even making sure he was destroyed, I staggered out onto the road and down to the harbor, still clutching the bottle of wine.

"I got to the *Easy* and untied her but the pain in my right thigh was spreading through my entire leg. I remembered how fast we had seen some people turn and I panicked. I didn't want to be a zombie. I started the engine, got the *Easy* on course for the lighthouse and tied the wheel with a piece of cord. I couldn't be sure she was going to reach you but it was the only chance I had.

"I wrote you a note, telling you the time I'd been bitten. That way, you'd know when I was going to turn, assuming you knew about the faulty vaccine and the four days it took to turn. I went down to the storeroom and injected myself. I only wrote you that note so that you'd know when to kill me. I didn't think you'd use the information to save me." Tears welled up in her eyes. "Thank you, Alex."

I put my arms around her and she cried against my shoulder.

I held her tight and felt hot, stinging tears running down my cheeks.

# CHAPTER 22

**W**HEN I LEFT LUCY'S ROOM, Hart met me in the corridor. He wore the face of a man who was deeply concerned.

"What is it?" I asked him.

"There's still no sign of Jax. We've scoured most of the island and all I have to show for it is the loss of a few good men to zombies. We can't have a Type 1 roaming the island and until the situation is dealt with, the director is going to be giving me hell about it." He pointed to a set of stairs. "She's asked to meet you. Come with me."

I followed him up the stairs to the reception area, then into the elevator and up to level 5.

"What does the director want with me?" I asked Hart as we stepped out of the elevator.

He shrugged. "I don't know. She asked me to get you, Tanya, and Sam. They're already in her office."

LIGHTNING

He led me to a door and knocked on it. A woman's voice said, "Enter."

We went into an office that was large but furnished in the same basic manner as the offices at Site Alpha Two. A bookshelf lined one wall and a desk sat near the window. The main difference between this room and the ones I had been inside at Alpha Two was a large oval meeting table. Sam and Tanya sat at the table, along with a woman in her fifties. She stood up when we entered and came over to shake my hand.

"You must be Alex. I'm Marilyn MacDonald, the director of this facility. Nice to meet you."

We shook. She was tall and slender and dressed for business in a dark trouser suit. Her blonde hair was pinned back and she wore glasses. Her face didn't betray any emotion, and I had the feeling that she could be cold and emotionless when she needed to be. In her line of business —running a government facility whose sister site had been responsible for the zombie outbreak—I supposed there were a lot of times that she needed that trait.

"Come and join us, Alex," she said, indicating a seat at the table next to Sam. I took it. MacDonald remained standing.

"You people have surprised me with your resourcefulness and skills," she said. "When Ian told me he was sending you to Site Alpha Two to recover the H1NZ1, I was skeptical to say the least. Yet here you are."

179

"Not all of us," Sam said. I looked at him closely. His eyes were bloodshot and I wondered if he had been crying.

"That's right, not all of you," MacDonald said. "Two of your number have been lost and that is regrettable. If it's any consolation, the chemical you brought back from Alpha Two will enable us to save many lives. Your friends did not die in vain."

It wasn't much of a consolation. I was glad that Lucy was recovering and that there was now an antivirus, but that didn't make the loss of Johnny or Jax any easier.

None of us replied to MacDonald so she continued. "I'll come straight to the point. This facility is in a dire situation. We are now responsible for producing the antivirus that can save everyone from becoming a zombie or a hybrid. That is a huge task yet we are trying to perform it with a skeleton staff. Once the virus is being manufactured in large quantities, we will need skilled and resourceful people such as yourselves to help us get it to the camps on the mainland."

"The army camps, you mean?" I asked.

"No, I mean the Survivors Camps."

Tanya leaned forward in her chair. "When you made the original vaccine, it was only being distributed to the army. Vaccinating the civilians didn't figure into your plans."

"It wasn't mean to happen that way," MacDonald said. "We sent the vaccine to the mainland. How the army distributed it was up to them."

LIGHTNING

"I've got a newsflash for you, man," Sam said. "They kept it for themselves."

"Yes, I am aware of the situation with the vaccine." MacDonald folded her arms. "As I said, that is not what we intended to happen. With the antivirus, we can do things differently if you help us. We don't have the resources to make sure the antivirus gets to the people in the Survivors Camps and I can't afford to spare the guards from the island. They have a tough enough job to do already keeping this facility safe."

"So you want us to do the job for you," Sam said. "What are you going to inject us with this time to make sure we do your bidding?"

"Nothing. We couldn't inject you even if we wanted to; you've all received the antivirus. You can't be turned. Besides, I wouldn't have thought that would necessary; I've looked into your backgrounds. You are the type of people who want to make a difference. You wouldn't have taken over the Survivor Radio station and given that message to the people if that wasn't the case. And Alex," she said, looking at me, "you want to find your brother and parents. What better way to do that than by visiting the Survivors Camps?"

She had a point. Helping her was my best chance to find Joe and my parents. Not only that, I wanted to get that antivirus into as many people as possible so that the virus that had taken my friends could be destroyed. We needed to eradicate the zombies.

181

"Can I take your silence to mean you'll do it?" she asked when none of us said anything.

"I'll do it," I said.

"Me too," Tanya added.

Sam looked at us, and then at MacDonald. "I guess somebody has to make sure this is done right. Count me in, man."

"Excellent." MacDonald smiled but I couldn't detect any genuine warmth in it. "You really are good people."

"We don't need your platitudes, lady," Sam said. "Just tell us what we need to do."

"It will take us a few days to manufacture enough of the antivirus for the first distribution run," she said. "We'll work out the details then. In the meantime, I'll get someone to assign you rooms and you can enjoy the few comforts our facility has to offer."

"Screw that," Sam said. "I'll be sleeping on the *Escape*."

I nodded. The thought of staying here at the facility didn't appeal at all. Especially when my home, *The Big Easy*, was so close. I wanted nothing more than to get onboard with Lucy and sail out onto the waves. The atmosphere at Apocalypse Island was oppressive, and I needed to escape it.

"That's fine of course," MacDonald said. "So we'll meet again in three days. By then the first batch of antivirus should be ready." She went to her desk and sat, indicating that the meeting was over.

LIGHTNING

Hart led us out of the room and toward the elevators. "Good to have you working with us again," he said as he jabbed the elevator button.

"At least this time we get a choice," I said.

He ignored that and said, "I'll get a team together to take you to the docks."

I pointed to the Desert Eagle on my hip. "I suppose you'll want this back."

Hart shook his head. "Keep it. You're going to need it when you take that antivirus to the mainland."

Tanya raised an eyebrow. "So you trust us not to sail away with your weapons?"

"Of course," Hart said. "As the director said, you're good people. You'll be back here in three days, I'm certain of it."

# CHAPTER 23

ART ARRANGED FOR A CONVOY of three Jeeps filled with men and women from his security team to drive us to the dock. The guards were all armed with automatic rifles and sat in the vehicles scanning the terrain as we drove beyond the gate. With Jax on the loose somewhere, these people weren't taking any chances.

We got to the dock without incident. I breathed a sigh of relief when I saw *The Big Easy* and *The Lucky Escape* waiting for us.

I told Lucy to get aboard while I untied the *Easy*. Although Lucy seemed perfectly fine and had regained her strength, I didn't want her to do anything strenuous, at least for a while. We had both been through a lot to be reunited and now that we were together again, I wanted to protect Lucy from everything, even the chance that she might pull a muscle untying the boat. My

LIGHTNING

overprotectiveness would probably drive Lucy mad sooner rather than later but for now, I wanted to do everything for her.

As I jumped from the dock onto the aft deck, I said, "Home, sweet home."

Lucy looked up at the sun. The day was unusually warm. "I'm going to put on a bikini and catch some rays on the sun deck."

"I approve," I said.

She kissed me. "And why don't you find a pair of shorts and catch some rays yourself?"

"I might do that," I said, surprising myself. I usually wore a baggy T-shirt no matter how hot it was. I had always tried to hide my body, but now I thought what the hell? I'd survived zombie attacks, explosions, being shot at, and an injection of the pure virus; being seen without a T-shirt wasn't going to kill me.

I climbed up to the bridge, picking up the radio and hailing *The Lucky Escape* while I sat in the familiar pilot's chair.

Sam answered. "What is it, man?"

"Any particular place you want to go?" I asked him.

"I don't care where it is, as long as it's far enough away from here that we can't see the island, man. Why don't we find a nice spot, just drift for a while, and enjoy the ocean and the freedom?"

"Sounds good," I said. "Lead the way."

185

Two hours later, we were drifting on the gentle waves. The coast was in sight, the cliffs bright in the sunlight. The wind was almost nonexistent, making the sun feel even hotter. Lucy was lying on the sun deck wearing one of the bikinis I had taken from the marine shop in Swansea, a yellow number that barely covered anything. I was in a pair of black board shorts, and nothing else, feeling comfortable and cool. We had Survivor Radio on. The new DJ wasn't a patch on Johnny. He played some good tunes, though. The opening bars of "Don't You Forget about Me" by Simple Minds drifted from the radio.

"Have you seen The Breakfast Club?" I asked Lucy.

She laughed. "Only two million times."

"We should get a DVD player," I suggested. "The next time we go shopping, we should get a DVD player and some movies."

"Sounds good to me, as long as we can get The Notebook."

"Ugh," I said. "Forget I mentioned it."

She looked at me with one eyebrow raised. "You haven't even seen it, have you?"

"No, and that's how it should be. You want a drink?"

"Sure. In fact, that bottle of wine I got from the village is in the storeroom."

"Sounds good." I went in through the door that led to the living area and kitchen. As I walked past the dining table and over to the door that led to the lower level, I noticed that it was open. That was strange; I was sure I had closed it.

Outside, Lucy screamed.

I ran for the door, scooping up the Desert Eagle from the kitchen table on the way. I yanked the gun from the holster and emerged onto the sun deck with it clutched in my hands, safety off.

Lucy was shrinking back toward the door, her eyes locked on the creature that stood on the deck.

It was Jax. She was naked, a map of dark veins visible beneath her skin. She glared at us with yellow eyes. Now I knew why the hunting parties hadn't been able to find her in the woods; she had been hiding out on the boat. But why had she waited so long before she made her presence known? I looked at the distant cliffs and the answer became obvious. The shore. She wanted to get to the mainland. I couldn't allow that to happen.

I wanted to talk to her; to see if any shred of the Jax I had once known was inside that monster somewhere.

"Jax," I said. "You don't have to do this."

She grinned at me with the same cruel grin I had seen on Vess's face at Site Alpha Two and lunged forward.

I shot the Desert Eagle twice in quick succession. The sound ripped through the air. The gun bucked twice in my hand. Jax fell backward over the railing and into the sea.

I rushed to the railing and looked overboard. There were ripples where she had hit the water, but no sign of her.

Sam shouted to me from the deck of the *Escape*. "What happened, man?"

"It was Jax," I replied.

"Did you shoot her?"

I remembered how Vess had moved so quickly that Johnny's bullet had missed him. "I don't think I hit her," I said. "I think she went over the side on purpose." I looked toward the mainland and pointed. "That's what she wanted all along, to get to the shore. We just gave her a lift to where she wanted to go."

Sam looked at the gentle sea and shook his head. "Man, it's gonna be bad if she's loose on the mainland."

I looked toward the distant cliffs and nodded. It was going to be bad.

It was going to be very bad.

Lucy appeared beside me and put her arms around my waist. "Don't beat yourself up over it, Alex. You tried to stop her."

"Yeah," I said.

\*\*\*

Later, after darkness had descended and Lucy and I had gone to bed and made love, I went back up to the living area and switched on the light over the easy chair. Taking a pen and a blank journal from the drawer. I poured myself a glass of the red wine that Lucy had risked her life to get, sat in the chair, and began to write about Apocalypse Island and Site Alpha Two and the loss of my friends.

By the time I was done, the sun was rising over the horizon, staining the sky orange and red. I stretched wearily in the chair, my bleary eyes looking down at the last words I had written:

*"Yeah," I said.*

I wished I could have said more to Lucy, assured her that everything was going to be all right. But I couldn't. Delivering the antivirus to the people on the mainland was going to be dangerous. With Jax on the loose, it was probably going to be even more dangerous. The zombies and hybrids were bad enough, but now an even more terrible monster roamed the land.

I rubbed my eyes. I needed to get back to bed. I might as well put Jax and the other creatures out of my mind for a while and enjoy the three days I had before we returned to Apocalypse Island.

Because these were probably the last good days I was ever going to have.

I turned off the light and went down to bed.

# Mailing List

If you would like to be informed of new releases, please
sign up for the Harbinger of Horror mailing list.
http://eepurl.com/OKFY9

Printed in Great Britain
by Amazon.co.uk, Ltd.,
Marston Gate.